The Spy Who Couldn't Count

The Spy Who Couldn't Count

Michael N. Wilton

Contents

Chapter One

Thick and Proud of It

It may be of some consolation to those who were not particularly bright at school, that there are others in the same boat who do not appear to have suffered unduly from the experience. But anyone like Jyp who had the misfortune to be educated at Watlington County Grammar was not expected to show any evidence of intellectual output. They were simply thick as planks and quite proud of it.

Although the headmaster talked expansively about Watlington's long and glorious history at the drop of a hat, and constantly referred to the string of famous old boys who were to be found listed on the honours board in the Great Hall, he was always coy about his other former pupils who exercised more unusual talents, such as robbing banks or selling London Bridge to trusting American tourists.

Despite the not unexpectedly low exam results every year, the school earned a certain fashionable notoriety as the worst school in the south-east, and parents liked to boast about their schooldays there. How awful it had been, and what happened to that bounder, what's-his-name, who pulled off that bank robbery and ended up in South America or somewhere.

None of them would, of course, admit even privately to themselves that school had been a complete waste of time, and that the chances of any of them getting on in the world, or winning any sort of public recognition for their services were remote in the extreme. That was before anyone had heard of Jyp.

Not that Jyp had any idea of making a name for himself. With a name like Jefferson Youll Patbottom, he felt he had already been burdened with more than his fair share of bad luck - which explains how he accepted his nickname so readily in the first place.

The simple explanation is that whereas most of the others at his school couldn't think, Jyp couldn't count. He never had been able to, and as far as he could see, he never would. Which may explain why he ended up working for the Civil Service.

When his father, George, heard about it, he simply couldn't contain himself and roared with laughter.

'You - in the Civil Service?' he gasped. 'You've got to be joking. What sort of work are you doing there?'

Jyp pulled at his nose in some embarrassment. 'Statistics...'

'Statistics?' choked his father, with rising disbelief. 'What kind, for Pete's sake? You can't even add two and two together!'

'Birth, marriages and deaths - that sort of thing.'

The news proved too much for his father. He looked around the room waiting for someone to tell him it wasn't true, then collapsed in his chair, wheezing with laughter. He rocked backwards and forwards, his face turning purple, until it looked as if he was going to have a seizure, and for a moment Jyp thought he would have to revise his mortality statistics for England and Wales.

'Maud,' his father called out weakly at last, wiping his eyes and making his way blindly to the kitchen to seek out an appreciative audience. 'Listen to this, it's a corker. D'you know what your son's gone and done this time? They've made him a Civil Servant. He's the one they're relying on to tell 'em how many people we've got in the country. Blimey, I don't know why they don't get him to count up the number of Civil Servants there are - we're knee deep in them already!'

Jyp tried not to listen and pushed the cat away moodily.

'It's all right for you, Rosy,' he groaned, hearing a burst of muffled laughter in the other room. 'All you do is feed your face all day. You don't have to add up columns and columns of perishing figures until your eyes pop out.'

Rosy stretched herself languidly, and jumped on his lap, demanding instant attention.

'Give over, Rosy.' He shook her off again, wondering vaguely why his mother couldn't call her pets unflowery names like anyone else, and mentally kicked himself for letting slip about his job. He wished he'd never mentioned it. With a juicy tit-bit like that to impart, his father would be full of it when he met his old pals down at the British Legion and it would be all over the village by the morning.

'Why did I have to have a joker for a father?' he asked the cat. 'Most ordinary fathers go to sleep in front of the telly when they get home, but not our dad - all he wants is a straight man for his double act. And guess who that is?'

But Rosy had her own problems, and started washing her front paws. As far as Jyp could remember, his father had always been the life and soul of the party, determined to see the funny side of everything. His mother, bless her, was loving and a bit scatter-brained at times, but she had lots of patience. Just as well, he thought, she has a lot to put up with.

A few minutes later she popped her head round the door and re-garded him sympathetically.

'You've gone and done it now, Jyp. Whatever made you tell him such a thing - you know what he's like?'

'Sorry, Mum,' sighed Jyp. 'I should have guessed what he'd say.'

Maud ruffled his hair. 'What made you pick a funny old job like that, anyway? You've never been keen on figures before. Not even the other kind.'

Jyp was slightly taken aback.

'You were always poking around in corners, playing with your stamps and things, never girls.'

'I tried to get a job in stamp collecting, Mum, but they found out I didn't know the difference between a Pfennig and a Schilling.'

'But we don't use that old fashioned currency anymore, silly,' said his mother lovingly. 'It's all new pence now.'

There was a sigh as Jyp tried again.

'I know that, Mum, but there aren't many jobs you can get without counting, these days,' he admitted sheepishly. 'I thought I was onto a good thing washing up dishes at the local restaurant, but I made so many mistakes working out the breakages, I ended up owing them money.'

'What about that job as a night watchman at the clock repairers? That didn't need any counting, did it?'

Jyp winced at the memory. 'No, but I knocked off one night earlier than I should have done, and some bright spark broke in and cleaned the place out. The manager told me to get a new alarm and when I asked him to give me one, he gave me the sack instead.'

He pondered on the sheer injustice of it all.

His mother looked puzzled. 'How did you get this job in the Civil Service then?'

Jyp took a deep breath. 'Well, it all started when I was leaning up against a wall having my lunch break at the Wall of Death, and this man came along...'

'Wall of Death?' repeated his mother faintly. 'That sounds rather dangerous.'

'No,' Jyp reassured her. 'They just ride around and around inside this bowl-shaped place. It's dead easy, like falling off a log. Well, perhaps not exactly like that,' he allowed. 'Anyway, all I had to do was to go and flag them in, now and then, so that someone else could take over. The only trouble was, I forgot to tell them one day 'cause I got the times mixed up, and one of them got tired and fell off. He was a bit cross,' he remembered reflectively.

'But why did you have to lean against the wall to have your sandwiches?' asked his mother, her mind running off at a tangent.

Jeff disregarded her question. 'He got his own back by tying me onto the front of his handle bars the next time he did his act.' He shuddered at the recollection. 'I couldn't sit down for weeks afterwards.'

'But why...?'

A hunted look appeared on Jyp's face. 'Look, Mum, why don't you let me tell the story my own way, otherwise I'll never get through it?'

'Sorry, Jyp.' His mother sat back obediently.

'Anyway, this man I was telling you about,' went on her son doggedly. 'He asked me to hold a bit of string for a minute and never came back. So I followed the line and found someone at the other end. He was so chuffed I'd stopped him wasting his time he offered me a job to help him out, doing his deliveries for him.'

He hesitated and seeing his mother smother a yawn went on quickly, 'Before I knew where I was, I'd lost my way. I asked a policeman and he found I had enough drugs on me to start up my own business. Mr Big the sergeant called me. I don't think he meant it, Mum. He said I hadn't got the brains for anything that smart, and they let me off with a caution. Anyway, it gave me an idea, and I decided to team up with George, down the road, in a travel agency. You are following me, Mum?'

'Mmm?' His mother jerked her head back with an effort. 'Er, yes, of course.'

'Right, well we did so well that George decided he couldn't wait for an accountant to work out our profits - he nipped off to the West Indies with all the money.' He added bitterly, 'He could count.'

His mother nodded her head in sympathy and tried to concentrate.

'When I reported it to the police, I got the same sergeant who pinched me with the drugs, and all he said was I was one of life's losers. He was dead right. So that's when he put in a good word for me to become a prison warder. Said it would give me a purpose in life, helping others.' He paused. 'It may have helped others, but it didn't help me.'

There was a muffled snort and his mother woke up. 'What happened then?' she asked automatically.

'They got rather upset 'cause I reported back with ten prisoners after a trip to the laundry one day.'

'What's wrong with that?' His mother smiled indulgently. 'Nothing wrong with your counting this time, was there?'

Jyp snorted. 'He says I took fifteen out with me.'

His mother rallied. 'It could have happened to anyone. Was that when you joined the Girl Guides?'

'Men aren't allowed to join the Girl Guides, Mum,' he explained patiently. 'I told you that before. I was at a fancy dress party, and there was a... misunderstanding.' He wriggled uncomfortably. 'I told you ages ago.'

'Well, they didn't have to lock you up,' she defended him stoutly. 'I wish I'd have been there, I'd have told them a thing or two. Anyway, what's that to do with the Civil Service?'

'There was this girl I borrowed the dress from for the fancy dress party. She told me about this vacancy in her office. Her name's Patience.'

'That's nice,' his mother beamed vaguely. 'I had a budgie called Patience once.'

'She was very nice to me. Told me where to go and what to say. I'd never have got the job with old Benson without her help.'

'Never mind love, you've got a job for life now – no more putting up with funny old lodgings. You're back home where you belong. Fancy, who'd have thought you'd end up with the Civil Service. What's your new boss like?'

A cloudy look passed over his face at the thought of his boss.

'I suppose some people like him, but he's a funny old cove. Mind you, most of them are in that place. Suppose it's something to do with counting figures all day. Not like Patience. She couldn't do enough for me. Can't understand it. Even her family's nice as well. Keep on asking me round for supper. You remember Aunt Ethel, Mum? The one you said was so fat they mistook her for a barrage balloon in the war? Well, I wouldn't call Patience fat exactly, but she's certainly well made.' He hesitated. 'She always wants me to kiss her, as soon as I get in the office.' There was a silence as he struggled with the next question. 'Mum, did you ever know anyone with a moustache - Mum?'

He peered forward eagerly, hoping for advice, but his mother was fast asleep.

* * *

Later that night, he woke up in a sweat, as realisation swept over him. 'They'll all know about it on the train tomorrow now. What am I going to do?' He groaned. 'Why couldn't I learn to count like anybody else?' Then he started. 'Oh, blimey. I forgot to give old Benson those figures yesterday. I wonder if I can get Patience to do them? He's bound to complain about them, he always does.'

He tossed and turned and eventually fell asleep, trying to count sheep and getting a different total every time. One of these days, he murmured to himself, you'll get a job that doesn't need figures. The only trouble was, he couldn't think of a single one.

Chapter Two

Strange Urges

'Now, you're not to get upset about all this, darling,' said his mother next morning, fussing over him as he was trying to leave. She straightened his tie and picked a cat hair off his shoulder. 'I'm sure you're imagining it.'

Jyp frowned. 'No, it was a cat hair. I just saw you take it off.'

'Silly boy, I mean this business about your new job. You know your father wouldn't talk about it to anyone else.'

'Oh, yes? Was I imagining it when the postman handed me next door's post this morning and said he couldn't even read our number?' said Jyp, smoothing back his unruly hair back in agitation and jumping nervously at a knock on the door.

'Don't worry, it's only the milkman.' She put her head out. 'There you are, what did I tell you. Hello, Jim.'

'Morning, Mrs Patbottam.' He grinned knowingly at the sight of Jyp.

'Now, Jim, you know we only have one - not three. What's the matter with you this morning? Not like you at all.'

'Sorry, missus.' He took two pints back with a laugh. 'We can't all be good at counting, can we? Bye now.'

Jyp quivered. 'You see! I told you, Dad went down to the British Legion last night.'

His mother patted his arm reassuringly. 'It's just a silly old coincidence. Now get off to work, otherwise you'll be late. What would your boss say then?'

Looking upset, Jyp jammed his hat on. 'Probably ask me why I bothered to come in, as usual.' He looked moodily along the road. 'I won't be able to look anyone in the face now. I bet they'll be full of it on the train.'

'What nonsense you do talk. I don't suppose anyone will take any notice of you. They'll all be too worried about catching it on time. And if you don't hurry, you'll miss it too.'

'Don't care if I do,' he muttered setting off slowly. He aimed a kick at the lamp post as he passed. 'At least you don't have to worry about what time to light up - it's all done for you.'

As he turned in at the station approach, he heard a snigger from a group standing near the entrance. Someone shouted, 'Don't forget to put the clock back tomorrow!' And a voice piped up, 'Better get a calculator.'

The train was full to the brim as usual. In the scrum to get on board, Jyp pushed and shoved with the rest to lever himself in. Just then, Jack, the porter bustled up waving his flag, anxious to get the train away.

'Hurry up, get in, sir.' He called inside. 'Now move along, room for one more. Oh, morning Mr Jyp, I can count on you to sort them out, can't I? Ha-ha.'

With his face jammed in the back of a large beefy woman in thick tweeds, Jyp could hardly see a thing during the first half of the journey and spent his time torturing himself, wondering what people were saying behind his back. Every little chuckle made him squirm until the woman in front turned round indignantly and asked him what he thought he was doing. In doing so, she sent the other passengers staggering in all directions. Luckily, at East Croydon, the carriage half emptied as some of the more athletic city types changed trains and sprinted for a London Bridge connection.

Immersed in gloom, Jyp automatically sat down on the only seat remaining and left the woman fuming. At that, a military gentleman in pinstripes got up and offered the beefy woman his place, giving Jyp an icy glance before trying to read his paper whilst hanging onto the luggage rack. Oblivious to the glares, Jyp soon got bored and started reading snippets of news from the newspaper in front of him. Some of the items were so interesting, he asked the person opposite to turn back the page so that he could have another look, but the man lowered the paper with an indignant rustle and exchanged outraged glances with the military gentleman still battling with the motion of the train. By the time the train pulled into Victoria, Jyp found he had a stiff neck from constantly turning his head sideways and reading at a funny angle. He was still massaging his neck while fumbling for his ticket at the barrier.

'Thank you, sir,' said the ticket collector, glancing at it. 'Oh, Watlington, eh? Isn't that where they've got that funny bloke who can't count?'

'Really?' uttered Jyp faintly, and tottered past.

* * *

As he scurried into the office, he heard a voice bellowing in the distance and dropped his hat in a panic.

'Pratbottam!'

'Oh, my God, it's old Benson.'

He looked around desperately for a way to escape, but left it a fraction too late. As if sniffing his presence, Mr Benson burst out of a door marked 'Head of Statistics' and bore down on him with a thunderous expression.

'Where are my death figures, Pratbottam?'

'Er, they're... they're in the other office, Mr Benson. Patbottam,' he corrected automatically.

'Well, get them, Patbottam. I've been waiting for them the past half hour. They should have been on my desk yesterday, as you know full well.'

'I'll bring them to you right away, sir.'

'Don't bother, I'll come and fetch them. Otherwise I'll be adding another one to the figures - yours. Hurry, man, hurry. Patbottam,' he snorted, as he watched him hurrying off. 'I was right the first time.'

Jyp led the way to his desk casting a stricken glance around the office for Patience, but her desk was unoccupied. He shuddered and went through the motions, turning over his papers.

'They're not there, are they, Pratbottam, or whatever your name is?' trumpeted Mr Benson. 'Right, that's it...'

Jyp stood rooted to the spot, his mind frozen, unable to think up any more excuses. He opened his mouth soundlessly, like a goldfish.

'Well, what have you got to say?' thundered his tormentor.

'Excuse me, Mr Benson, are these the figures you were looking for?' A demure voice broke the spell and Mr Benson, looking thwarted, snatched at them.

'Ah, Patience, I might have guessed you wouldn't let me down. Why can't you be like her, Pratbottam? Someone I can rely on, all the time.'

'But, Mr Benson, I didn't prepare these.' Patience looked up at him earnestly.

'No?' Mr Benson's fingers began to twitch, a sure sign his blood pressure was rising.

'No.' She smiled sweetly. 'Mr Patbottam asked me to type them out for him yesterday - that's why they're so late. I'm afraid it's all my fault.'

Jyp let out a strangled sigh of relief.

Mr Benson shot him a look of brooding suspicion. 'Oh, I see. Right then. Looks as if I'll have to let you off this time.' He turned away reluctantly. 'See that it doesn't happen again, or else.'

As his footsteps died away, Jyp subsided limply into the nearest chair.

'Don't I get a little something for being so good?' cooed Patience, leaning over him, blotting out the light. 'Oh, Jyp,' she cried passionately, pressing his face in her vast enveloping bosom, leaving him gasping for air.

Re-focusing his eyes, Jyp smiled uncertainly. 'Ta, ever so, Patience.'

For a moment, Patience stood there beaming, then making up her mind she waddled over to her desk and extracted a bag coyly from the bottom drawer.

'Oh, here's a copy of those figures.'

'Thanks.' Jyp stuffed them carelessly in his pocket with the air of a man who's passed through the storm and was gently relaxing with nothing to fear from anyone.

Taking advantage of the opportunity, Patience pulled out an unrecognisable object. 'I bet you don't know what I'm doing, Jefferson, dear.'

'No, what is it, Patience?' asked Jyp straightening himself out after the onslaught.

'I'm doing a little knitting.'

'That's nice.'

'D'you know what it's going to be?'

'No, surprise me.'

Patience it held it up against herself. 'Go on, have a guess.'

Jyp glanced up idly from a book he was reading and made a puzzled guess at the lengthy unfinished woollen garment she was looking at lovingly.

'A football supporter's scarf?'

'No... think of bells.'

'A bell ringing scarf?'

A strained smile appeared on her face. 'You remember what you said to me at the last office party, Jefferson, dear?'

Jyp thought for a moment. 'No?'

'It was awfully romantic.'

'Was it when I emptied the brandy into Mr Benson's punch when he wasn't looking?'

'No, you're not concentrating, Jefferson. It was about us...'

As Jyp continued to look blank, Patience dropped a hint.

'It's a wedding dress...'

'Is someone getting married?' He looked fogged.

'Oh, Jefferson. I think you do it on purpose. You are an old tease. Look,' she fished out a piece of paper from the bag. 'I used a pattern out of 'Tomorrow's Women'. Don't you think it would go with that blue and orange suit you wore on New Year's Eve?'

'I don't think you could wear it with my suit, Patience.'

He couldn't remember whether it was the fifth murder he was reading about, but as he caught the expression in Patience's eyes he had some idea how the victim must have felt.

'I wasn't proposing to wear the suit, dearest. You are.'

Jyp's mouth fell open as the significance of her conversation began to strike him. He was about to tell her it was the suit her dog was sick over when he caught sight of the paper she handed over.

'What's this, some sort of application?' he asked brightly. 'Oh, look, it's got our names on it. And they've spelt my name right for a change.' He looked up, smiling nervously.

'That's right, dearest, I made it out for us, so we could get fixed up at the registry office before the Bank Holiday rush starts.'

'Fancy, a registry office. I've never been a witness before. Is it anyone we know?'

'Oh, Jefferson, how could you!' Her soft dewy eyes blazed with indignation, and she seemed to swell up in front of him with such pent up emotion she would have been snapped up instantly by a producer casting for a starring role in a wartime epic about barrage balloons. Controlling herself with a supreme effort, Patience decided that the time for shilly shallying was over. It was now or never.

'We are getting married - next week, my dearest,' she cooed. 'You and me. In a registry office. You proposed at the party and I accepted.' She grabbed him as he started sliding down out of the chair with a dazed expression. 'You called me your little fairy, I shall always remember that.'

'Married?' Jyp stammered. He rallied in desperation. 'There's been some mistake. I-I didn't call you a fairy.'

'You did, my darling. Oh yes, you did,' she spoke firmly, bearing down on him with the determination of a Sherman tank advancing on enemy lines.

'No, no...' He searched around frantically. As his eye fell on her knitting pattern, he cried out with a flash of inspiration. 'I meant *I* was a fairy, not you. Me.' He took fresh heart as she paused in astonishment. 'You see, I'm not like other men - I have these strange...urges. I go completely out of control. If you must know,' he shut his eyes and sent up a prayer for help.

'What I really wanted to do at the party, was to...er...wear your dress.'

'My - what?'

While she was still reeling from the shock, Jyp scrambled to his feet and felt wildly behind him for the door handle.

'I don't know how to tell you this, but ever since I first met you all I wanted to be was...a woman, just like you.' He winced at the ghastly thought it conjured up, and dived at the door as her mouth opened wide and her screams followed him down the corridor.

Chapter Three

Only a Couple of Hundred

Crouching in the dark with his fingers jammed tight in his ears, Jyp imagined he could still hear the screams echoing down the corridor. The next minute the door was flung open letting in a bright shaft of light, almost blinding him.

"Ere,' bellowed a voice. 'Wot you doing in the broom cupboard?'

Peering out fearfully, Jyp recognised the bearded figure of Ted, the hall porter, and sighed with relief. He extricated his fingers with difficulty, and pulling his foot out of a bucket climbed out sheepishly.

'Ah, Ted. Door seems to have got stuck.'

He cast a feverish look along the corridor and seeing it empty, gabbled the first thing that came into his head. 'Just looking for some figures. Not important, really. No.'

'You won't find her in there,' cackled the elderly porter. 'I heard Miss Patience organising a posse to come and look for you. Screaming her head off, she were.'

Jyp shuddered. 'Fine, fine. Must be one of her off days – nothing serious. Just…just don't tell her you saw me, eh, Ted?'

'No fear of that, young Jyp. She's been after me an' all in her time.'

Taking in the old man's white hair and wiry frame, Jyp patted his bony shoulder. 'Great, great, keep it up. Must dash.' He jumped nervously and started to edge away as a trolley appeared around the corner, followed by the tea lady.

Ted gave a sly grin and called after him, 'Saw you get on a number nine bus, didn't I?'

'I think I'll skip the tea, Ted,' decided Jyp with a gulp and made his escape. Rounding a bend in the corridor, he sighted another group of people in the distance, turned back and bolted in the opposite direction.

'There he is!' a cry went up, and they surged after him with whoops of delight, thinking they had their quarry cornered.

Jyp reversed in a mad panic and dived down a side turning, screaming inwardly. He spied a man entering a door ahead and dived after him, knocking him flying. Slamming the door closed he leaned back against it, panting.

The man, a tall military looking character, clambered to his feet looking ruffled. After straightening his suit he sat down behind a desk and as if seeing Jyp for the first time looked at his watch in surprise.

'I say, bit early, aren't you? That chap at Personnel said you'd been held up - trust them to get it wrong. Never mind.' Then trying to be more hospitable, he motioned to a chair. 'Take a pew. Lady Trench will be here in a minute. I'm Brigadier Sleuth, by the way. I know, bit silly having a name like that, seeing the type of work we do, but…ah, there you are, dear lady.'

A formidable tweedy figure marched in and to his horror Jyp remembered her as the woman in the train. 'Brigadier,' she nodded briskly, and checking her watch, turned to Jyp. 'Keen type, eh? Good, good. Let's get it over with - got a lot on today.' She settled herself into her seat, getting herself as comfortable as she could in her bulky jacket and thick army blanket type skirt, and peered uncertainly at Jyp. 'Haven't I seen you somewhere before?'

Jyp hurriedly pulled a face to put her off and listened nervously to the baying noise getting closer outside. Any moment now, they would be thumping on the door, asking if anyone had seen him. He was in such a state of nerves he sat there in a trance for a moment, almost losing track of the conversation, fearful of what might happen next.

'No? Never mind,' she said giving up. 'You go ahead with the technical stuff then, Brigadier. I'll follow up on the personnel side later.'

The Brigadier cleared his throat. 'Righto. Won't beat about the bush. Let's have your name, young fellow.'

'Patbottom,' said Jyp automatically, swivelling his head towards the door.

'Oh, incognito, eh? What do they call you in the Mess?'

Jyp had a mental vision of his father laughing his head off, and winced. 'Er, Jyp.'

'Ask a silly question, eh? Right then, Jyp, 'nuff said. Now you know why you're here. Won't beat about the bush. We're looking for a man with the right kind of experience and background for the work we have in mind. Hush hush, and all that. We're very fussy these days, after all the clangers we've had in the past, eh Prunella?'

Lady Trench nodded expressively and busied herself with her knitting, working on what looked like a cross between a bullet proof waistcoat and a mobile nuclear shelter. Jyp became so engrossed in the spectacle, he missed the Brigadier's opening remarks.

'...only ex-SAS considered - unless you have a very special sort of talent,' he rumbled. 'We want to see a man who's seen it all. Been through hell and back, if you like, and used to being under fire. Sounds familiar?'

Jyp replied feelingly. 'It happens all the time.' He leaned forward confidingly. 'That Mr Benson's been after me all day, all because I hadn't got his figures.'

'Benson?' A frown creased the Brigadier's forehead. 'Is he one of ours?'

'Well, he's not one of mine.' Jyp was positive on that one.

'KGB or the Mafia?'

Recalling the title on Benson's door, Jyp ventured, 'I think he's HOS.'

'Oh, one of the breakaway republics, I expect.' Dismissing the thought, the Brigadier went on keenly. 'What kind of figures?'

'Oh, Deaths, and things like that.'

In the electrified silence that followed, Jyp thought he'd better try to explain, but only succeeded in making matters worse. 'Mr Benson says I've killed off half the Home Counties since I've been there.' He laughed nervously. 'He exaggerates, of course. A couple of hundred, here and there, before lunch, perhaps.' Seeing their look of disbelief, he hurried on. 'Mistakes like that could happen to anyone. But I put it right before I leave every night. And if I don't, Patience usually helps out.'

'Patience?'

Seeing a confused look on his interrogator's face, Jyp became flustered.

'Well, she doesn't do it officially, if you know what I mean. It's only that lately she's been very helpful when Mr Benson wants something in a hurry.' There was a sharp intake of breath from Lady Trench and he floundered. 'That's why I popped in just now. She's been very... you know, pressing lately.' He laughed nervously. 'I must have upset her, though. She got so mad I thought she was going to kill me. That was them outside just now.'

'Kill you? Good grief! I thought she was on your side,' said the Brigadier looking dazed. 'And what about this Benson fellow?'

'Oh, he wants to kill me as well. But, he can't do that,' said Jyp happily, waving a sheet of paper. 'I've got his figures.'

'D'you mind, old chap?' The Brigadier reached across. He looked up astonished after scanning the list, his eyes popping out of his head.

'Are these deaths all yours? There seem to be rather a lot.'

'Oh yes, and that's only yesterday's.'

'Good Heavens! Doesn't it bother you - all this killing business?'

Jyp pondered for a minute, twisting about in his seat, trying to understand what the question meant.

'I don't see why it should. After all they're dead, aren't they. All I did was lay them out in columns, and add them up.'

'Where do you get all these figures? They're enormous. Looks more like battlefield casualties! Hang about, they're civilians. Where did they come from - somewhere in the Far East?'

'No, our office on the third floor.'

Jyp took the paper back from quivering fingers.

'I'm not supposed to show anyone these - they're confidential, you know.'

'I should think they are. I've never seen anything like it! Tell me, have you always been doing this sort of thing?'

Jyp squirmed. 'No, I once got a job at a sort of clock place, but that blew up on me.'

'Oh, time bombs, eh?'

'Then I was kind of keeping watch on some high speed motor bikes, but that fell through. They didn't always come back.'

'Ah, despatch stuff.'

'They called it the wall of death.'

'I should think so, too.'

'And the rest, well, I'd rather not talk about that.'

'I see, hush hush, eh? Well, it looks as if you've had an impressive career to-date, young Jyp. Doesn't look as if you've put a foot wrong.'

Looking coy, Jyp ventured, 'Oh, I wouldn't go so far as to say that. Fair's fair. If I got it wrong, Patience was always willing to help out. She's very good at persuading people, you know.'

'Is she now?' The Brigadier coughed. 'Which reminds me. What sort of um…persuader do you use?'

Jyp looked mystified for a moment, then his face cleared. 'Oh, you mean this?' He whipped a pen out of his pocket and pointed it at the Brigadier, who flinched. 'Useful thing, these gadgets, aren't they. Look, when I press that, it reloads all by itself.'

'Mind where you're pointing that, young man,' croaked the Brigadier, while his companion, oblivious, went on knitting. Wiping his forehead, he asked, fascinated, 'What happens if it gets stuck, or doesn't work?'

'Oh, I just rub them out,' said Jyp warming to the subject.

'Rub them out? What with?'

Jyp ran through his pockets. 'I've got it here somewhere. Wipes out whole columns in one go. Don't know what I'd do without it. Ah, here it is.' He lobbed a rubber over helpfully.

The Brigadier took one petrified look and disappeared under the table.

Breaking off her knitting, Lady Trench looked up. 'All finished? Good. Now, young man, I don't know anything about the technicalities of the job. All I want to know is - have you got any young gels into trouble?'

Jyp drew himself up. 'Certainly not.' Then uneasily, at the sound of marching feet outside, 'I'd better go, I think that's Mr Benson after me again.'

A galvanised Brigadier hoisted himself to his feet, brushing himself down, slightly embarrassed. 'Nonsense, my dear chap. Can't let a young fellow like you go, just like that. Couple of dozen, did you say? My word, Prunella, we could do with a few more like him, eh?'

Ignoring her look of doubt, the Brigadier clutched Jyp's shoulder and beamed. 'Here, take my card. Jyp, did you say? Report to that address tomorrow, first thing. Meanwhile, I'll show you a back way out so you can avoid that Benson fellow. I'll make sure he doesn't trouble you again. Oh, and you'd better let me have your address details before you go, just to keep our security people happy. Ah, good man,' he said, pocketing the information.

Satisfied, he unlocked a bookcase and, pressing a button, opened a door. 'Well, glad to have you with us, er Jyp. These days, we have to hang together, don't we. I say - I haven't met you before have I?'

Coming back and rubbing his hands, he crowed, 'What about that, eh, Prunella?'

Lady Trench snorted. 'You do realise, we know nothing about the man, Percy? Sounds a bit of an oddball to me - did you notice his eyes wander every time someone went past in the corridor?'

'I tell you, we could do with a few more oddballs like him in security,' said the Brigadier, settling back with a gratified look on his face. 'Jimbo tells me his office needs someone like that - if you only knew. Mum's the word, eh? Hrm, you're quite right, though. Better get him security vetted. You know, the usual thing.' He grew excited again. 'Can't wait to see old Jimbo's face when I tell him. Just the sort of chap we need for that new security post we're setting up down on the coast. Whew, a couple of dozen before lunch! Beats that Bond fella into a cocked hat, eh?'

Chapter Four

The Right Kind of Person

When news of the latest recruit reached Whitehall, two senior security officials poured over the details with mounting satisfaction.

'I say Binky, this seems to be just the fellow we were looking for.'

'Absolutely. First class, Trevor, old man, couldn't be better. Couple of dozen before lunch, eh? Now we're getting something. We can really get things off the ground.'

'Off the ground,' repeated the other dutifully. 'I say, that was a brilliant idea of yours setting up that security post at the coast. Now we can really check on things.'

'Thanks, old man – that's just what I thought.'

'No really, what made you think of it?'

'The idea just came to me – I get these flashes of inspiration from time to time.'

'Seriously, who would have thought of it? Now we can sort out the villains before they have a chance to get started. Wouldn't be surprised if you get awarded something special for this.'

'Awfully good of you, Trevor, old man. Though, fair's fair. I couldn't have done it without your help.'

'Think nothing of it, Binky – we're in this together, aren't we? Shoulder to shoulder and all that rot?'

'Don't think I haven't forgotten all your hard work either, Trevor.'

'Good of you to say so, Binky. I say, it was just as well MI6 roped us in on this lark, wasn't it? What with all those spies popping up all over the place. Poor dears, I don't know how they managed before we came along.'

'Well, don't forget that's what we're here for – Civil Service and all that rot.'

'We've certainly been very civil about it, eh what?'

'Well, I must say, it's all beginning to turn out as we hoped. I wonder how that new man will cope?'

'If he's as good as old Sleuth says, we don't have a thing to worry about.'

'Tell you what, I'd like to be in his shoes right now. I wonder what he's thinking?'

At that moment, Jyp was in the middle of a horrible dream, imagining he could still hear the shrill cries of Patience ringing in his ears. At the sound of the bedside alarm he sat bolt upright and wiped his forehead, relieved he was at last safe from her clutches. He decided, there and then, that the first thing he would do would be to search out that address the Brigadier had given him, and get himself out of the nightmare plaguing his existence for the past - he didn't know how many months - and somehow make a fresh start.

Grabbing a leftover sandwich and gulping down a cup of coffee, he threw on a jacket and set out. Scrutinising the note Brigadier Sleuth gave him, he dashed for the train, changed at East Croydon and waited for a Brighton connection that stopped at the nearest station to his destination at - what was the name of the place? He consulted the address again, that's it, Plumpton Green.

Sitting back in the carriage, he conjured up pictures in his mind about his destination. Plumpton Green – that was the place his dad's golfing friends at the Legion were always mad about. He could still remember snatches of their conversation whenever he had to fetch his father home worse for wear, after one of his drinking sessions. 'Right bang by the seaside and a green fit for a king,' they would say, and 'Just the place to park the wife and the kids on the beach while we make a beeline for the club.'

Getting there a bit late and checking the address again with a passer-by after leaving the train, he scratched his head and hailed a taxi, wondering what sort of place his new bosses would have chosen for a headquarters that would blend in with the surroundings. As soon as he paid off the taxi and turned to survey his new office he understood. He was confronted with a shop bearing a faded sign, 'Sportswear' and underneath a sign in the window, urging shoppers to 'Get your latest golfing gear from Jimbo'. Reassured that it was the same name the Brigadier had mentioned, Jyp opened the door, setting off a jangling bell at the back of the shop.

After repeated rings, a tousled head emerged, and a young man entered, hiding a yawn.

'Mmm, sorry about that. Can I help you, sir?'

Deciding to take a chance, in the hope of finding out something about the unusual set-up he found himself in, Jyp glanced around the empty shop and tried to cover up his nerves with a breezy approach, 'Business not booming at the moment?'

The young man grinned. 'You could say that. Can I be of any assistance, or are you just browsing?'

'Um...I was given this address - I've been told to ask for Jimbo.'

'Ah...' The tone became guarded. 'What name shall I say?'

'Patbottom – Jefferson Patbottom...'

The young man's face lit up in sudden recognition. 'Here, I know who you are - you must be Jyp!'

Jyp winced. 'Ah...um...yes. How did you know that?'

Now his identity was established the young man became quite chatty.

'Go on, you'll never guess. Try me.'

'Some sort of business connection?'

'No, go on, try again.'

'Friend of the family?'

'No, one more.'

Jyp sighed, after racking his brains. 'I give up.'

The young man nudged him triumphantly. 'Go on, you're having me on. I bet you knew all the time. My brother's your milkman - how about that?'

Jyp groaned inwardly and the other carried on cheerfully. 'Yes, I know, it's a small world, isn't it? Never thought we'd get someone like you coming along. Mind you, we get all sorts here – the last one thought he was Napoleon! And then there was that one who did a knife act on the stage before she came here.'

'What happened to her?' asked Jyp, fascinated despite himself.

'Oh, she had to give it up because of her eyesight. Mind you, she tried out the routine once or twice when she got here. Said she wanted to keep her hand in. We nearly lost the postman over that.' He became reflective. 'I suppose it's something to do with the job. Gets you at the end, don't it? Now where was I?' he broke off as Jyp stirred restlessly. 'Ah, yes, you want to see old Jimbo.' He leant over confidentially. 'If you take my advice, whatever you do, don't start talking about golf, or you'll never hear the last of it – potty about it, he is.' He straightened up as Jyp coughed pointedly. 'Yes, right then, if you'll follow me, it's up on the first floor, Room 13. I'd better lead the way - in case you get the numbers mixed up.' He gave a knowing laugh.

As they climbed up the last few steps he waved a hand. 'Here we are then, Room 13, straight ahead.' Indicating the number he joked, 'Unlucky for some they say – mind how you go.' Delivering a final word of advice, he added confidingly, 'Don't be alarmed if he waves a club at you – he's only practising. If it gets too much give us a shout and I'll come and rescue you. My name's Reg, by the way - everyone knows me. Wait a mo', I'll just stick my head in and see if the coast is clear.'

Looking over his shoulder, Jyp caught a glimpse of a young woman's head swivel around, looking startled at their entrance. Reg waved a hand reassuringly. 'Gent to see the boss, Miss Julie - a Mr Patbottom.' Then giving a thumbs-up, he winked and whispered encouragingly, 'He's one of us,' before ushering Jyp in.

'Thanks.' Jyp waited until his footsteps died away and eased himself into the reception, at the same time looking around cautiously, hoping the man he had come to see would be in a more receptive mood than the one his new friend had so colourfully described.

The receptionist waved at him, still listening to someone talking on her phone. As she hurriedly replaced the handset, Jyp caught the words, 'I'll send the money by courier tomorrow,' and the brusque reply, 'That's no good – I need it now,' and the line went dead.

'I'm sorry, what name did you say?' the receptionist went a shade pink after turning the speaker off, slightly embarrassed at being caught out.

'P-Patbottom,' stuttered Jyp, suddenly overcome at the sight of the vision before him. For love had come to Jyp when he least expected it, after his shattering experiences with Patience. But this was the real thing, and he was at a loss for words.

'Good morning, Mr Patbottom.' She flashed him a winning smile that made him go weak at the knees. 'I'll just see if the Major is expecting you. Perhaps you would take a seat while I enquire.'

Sitting awkwardly on the edge of his seat Jyp admired her trim figure as she got up from her desk and left the room, and couldn't help catching snatches of the following conversation that could be heard wafting from the inner office.

'Who did you say? Fancy sending that young feller down at this time in the morning – of all the damn silly things to do, when I'm expecting an urgent courier delivery, and I haven't finished my practice shots...I mean my morning brief – that blasted Sleuth's got no consideration. Why didn't you put him off, Miss Diamond?'

'But sir, Brigadier Sleuth said it was most urgent. He said he had the very man for you, and I know you were so anxious to get a replacement.'

'So I was, so I was. Damn it, there goes my call. Go and keep him talking – give him a few figures to add up to keep him busy.'

Emerging from the office and smiling brightly at Jyp, the receptionist picked up a sheet of papers off the desk without looking at them, and offered them apologetically. 'I do apologise. Major Fanshaw has just had an unexpected call – it happens all the time here, I'm afraid. He says he won't be long, and wondered whether you could spare the time to have a go at this little puzzle while you're waiting. It's just one of his games he likes to try out on people.'

'Of course, of course,' mumbled Jyp, immediately dropping the papers, unable to take his eyes off the vision in front of him, before nervously helping her gather them together again. Glancing distractedly at her neat figure as she crouched in front of him, and then at the figures as they danced up and down on the pages, he blurted out. 'What…what are these?'

'Oh, he said you'd know all about them – in your line of business,' she said distractedly, her head tilted on one side, listening. Hearing the tinkle of the phone, she excused herself quickly and walked back to her desk, carefully lifting up the handset, whilst smiling encouragingly at the bemused Jyp.

At the sound of the inner door opening, she quickly replaced the phone and busied herself at her laptop.

'Ah, Mr Pratbottom?' the Major boomed, advancing on Jyp. 'Sorry to be called away when you arrived - devilish busy this time of the year.'

Jyp uncoiled himself and upset the papers again. 'Not at all. Pleased to meet you, Major Fanshaw.'

The other brushed his moustache and coughed importantly. 'Major Fanshaw-Smythe, don't you know. People are always getting it wrong – bad for morale, you know.'

Before Jyp could think up a reply, the Major's eye caught sight of the figures and he beamed. 'Ah, got you on that lark, have we? Usual routine test you know, just to see how young fellers like you shape up.' He took a closer look at the total, and his smile froze. 'What's this? Four million? How the devil did you get that? It's supposed to be my golf round, not the national debt! Anyone would think you can't count!' He laughed at the absurdity, then sobered up at the expression on Jyp's face. 'Here, this will never do. We can't just take on any old recruit who turns up, can we? We do have certain standards, don't we Miss Diamond? We'd look perfect idiots otherwise, dammit,' as he struck a pose with his favourite iron for comfort.

'Of course not,' agreed Jyp, swallowing.

'I know,' the Major burst out with a flash of inspiration, 'let's do a quick count, and see how you get on with something else – test the old mental reflexes, eh?' He prodded Jyp, 'Tell me, what does 49 and 52 come to – that was my last round,' he added modestly.

'Um... 150?' Jyp hazarded a guess wildly.

'Good God. How did you get that? Think again. Let's try something simple then. What about five plus six?'

Seeing his anguished face, the secretary held up two fingers behind the Major's back.

'Two?' he guessed tentatively.

'What?' The Major's face was beginning to turn purple. 'Are you sure they sent the right man, Julie?'

In the background, the receptionist hurriedly held up crossed fingers and added a single.

Jyp gulped and tried again. 'Eleven?'

'Hrm, I should damn well think so. Now then,' sizing him up. 'Let's see what you're made of. Stand up... no, over here,' as Jyp instinctively moved closer to the secretary.

The Major looked Jyp up and down. 'Stand up straight, man. Here, hold this,' handing him his golf club. 'Let's see you tee up.'

'I've had a drink, thanks,' said Jyp, confused.

'I mean, how you address the ball,' ordered the Major impatiently.

'Hello?' attempted Jyp, completely lost.

The receptionist smothered a giggle in the background, and hastily turned it into a cough.

'No, dammit, come over here and stand up straight. That's better,' grudgingly. 'Your stance is not bad – could be better. Right, let's see how you go about it.'

At Jyp's blank reaction, the Major took over. 'No, no, no. Watch me and see how it's done.' He seized the club and stood back. 'See that?

This is how you stand. Get the stance right. Hold the club like this, head still, don't sway your body and don't take your eye off the ball, and you can't go wrong. Now you try.'

He watched Jyp critically and shook his head. 'Well, we can't all be good at it right away, I suppose. Pity…now, what was it you came about, I forget.'

Miss Diamond coughed, and prompted discreetly in the background, 'Mr Patbottom is here about the vacancy, Major.'

'Ah yes, I'd better fill you in, Patbottom, hadn't I. It's like this,' he searched for the right words as he waggled the club. 'Hrm. Let me explain. We are a small dedicated body looking after security to see that only the right kind of person gets in. What we don't want are those bounders who think they've got every right to be here, like,' he waved his arms around, 'like those idiots who foozle about all over the place and miss their shots and break their clubs and push off thinking they own the place.' He straightened up indignantly. 'Over my dead body, I say. I shall fight to keep them out.' Breaking off, he caught caught sight of Jyp's bewilderment. 'Sorry, got carried away there, where was I?'

'You were about to tell Mr Patbottom what he is expected to do,' reminded his secretary gently.

'Ah, yes, well look here, Pratbottom, we don't expect you to do too much to start with, just a few simple tasks to help you get your eye in, as it were. Come back tomorrow and Miss Diamond here will show you the ropes, and run over the course with you. We keep a tight ship here, Pratbottom, don't forget, men's lives may depend on it. Be here at nine sharp in the morning - which reminds me.' He looked at his watch, 'I'm already late for my round, I mean appointment.' He turned to his secretary. 'I'll leave him in your good hands, Julie, so if you'll excuse me…'

As the door closed behind him, the secretary looked at Jyp apologetically. 'You must think we're a bit mad.'

'No, no,' Jyp assured her quickly, and looked at his watch, hesitating. 'I suppose it's a bit early, otherwise I'd be happy to…I mean I don't suppose you'd like to have a spot of lunch, or something.'

Taking pity on him, the receptionist smiled sympathetically. 'Well, it's a bit early. I was only going to have a sandwich break, but if you insist.'

'Oh, yes, please,' he said eagerly before she could change her mind. 'Is there somewhere around here?'

She laughed at his expression, and the lilt in her voice convinced him more than ever that he had at last found his true companion in life.

'There is a little cafe around the corner – it's nothing special but they know me there.' She apologised, 'I'm sorry, I haven't introduced myself, have I? I'm Miss Diamond – but call me Julie.'

'Julie,' repeated Jyp, savouring the name, and seeing her look of expectation blurted out. 'Everyone calls me, Jyp.'

'Hello, Jyp.' Then slightly embarrassed at his look of devotion, she picked up her purse.

'Shall we go there then?'

Finding his voice with an effort, Jyp stuttered, 'Right, let's go.'

* * *

Once settled and feeling bolstered by a steaming cup of coffee after tucking into a delicious quiche salad, Jyp took advantage of the Major's odd behaviour as an excuse to find out a little more about his companion. 'Is he always like that?' he tried hopefully.

Looking around to make sure they were not overheard, Julie took the plunge, 'I'm afraid so. I've never come across anyone quite so besotted with the game. But my dad did warn me that you have to be a bit mad to be in the game in the first place, and he should know.'

Noticing her hesitation, Jyp took her up on it. 'Why, is he in the same line of business?'

'He's retired now.' She took a second glance around, and whispered. 'He was in Special Branch,' as if that explained everything.

Slightly fogged, Jyp mulled it over. 'You mean, some branch of the police?'

'He was involved in security.'

A light shone in Jyp's mind. 'Is that why you were listening on the phone?'

Slightly embarrassed, Julie defended herself. 'I was only drafted in as a temp when I first started, but when I told Dad about some of the things going on in the office, he persuaded me to stay and asked me to keep an eye open and let him know of anything unusual.'

Anticipating his next unspoken question, she said hurriedly, 'He's still in touch with people in the know. Anyway,' she shook her head and changed the conversation, laughing, 'that's enough about me – how did you get into it, if it's not a rude question. Sounds as if you've led an exciting life so far, from what I've heard of it?'

Hesitating, afraid of making a fool of himself, thinking back over his past record, he caught a look of friendly sympathy on her face and decided to make a clean breast of it. 'I don't really know how it all happened,' he began, then it all came out with a rush.

About halfway through his recital, Julie stuffed a napkin in her mouth to stop herself collapsing into a fit of giggles, and finally after a supreme effort managed to pull herself together. 'And this friend of yours – Patience – is she still after you?'

'Where?' he turned around in a panic, mishearing her remark.

Hiding a smile, Julie reached out and tried to calm him down. 'I don't mean now. Is she still trying to get in touch with you – does she know where you are?'

He wiped his forehead. 'Not if I can help it. That's why I jumped at the offer.' Reflectively, 'I could wear a beard I suppose.'

'I don't think that would suit you,' she decided with a straight face. 'We'll just have to make sure she doesn't get to know – I'll warn Reg. He's a good friend if you get stuck or anything.'

Following up her train of thought, Jyp appealed, 'Anyway. What am I supposed to do? I don't know anything about security. That chap Sleuth got it all wrong – he thinks I'm some sort of super spy catcher.'

'Don't worry, Reg will guide you through it. Just get here at nine o'clock tomorrow as the Major said, and we'll put you on the "school run".'

'The school run?' echoed Jyp. 'What on earth's that?'

'It's a sort of beginner's introduction – everyone has to do it. You'll see, nothing to worry about. Now,' she consulted her watch, 'I must get back – otherwise the Major will be after me.'

'But wait, I don't understand. What do you mean – the school run...?'

As she opened her mouth to speak, a man with a cap pulled down over his eyes came in and sat down behind them.

At the sight of him, Julie froze. 'Tell you about it later,' she mouthed. Then in an unnaturally loud voice she exclaimed. 'Well, I must get back – I've a lot to do. See you in the morning.'

Jyp sat there for a while mulling over Julie's words, wondering who the man was and what would happen if he followed Julie's example. Would he be followed? Deciding to put it to the test, he half-heartedly started to get up and caught sight of the other man folding up his newspaper and fishing in his pocket for some small change ready to leave on the table. Blast! Jyp sank back again nervously, deciding to sit it out. As he pondered on his next step, the waitress took the decision out of his hands. Anxious to get the table cleared, she bustled up noisily loading the empty dishes on the table, enquiring pointedly, 'Another cup, dearie?'

'Mmm?' Jyp came to with a start.

The waitress consulted her watch. 'Only that we're expecting a big party about now, so if you don't mind?'

'Er, no, of course not, yes, I must get on.' As he rose reluctantly, he called after her inspired by a sudden thought, 'Am I near the bus stop here?'

'Yes, dear, down the road on the right – you can't miss it.'

Satisfied the remark had been overheard, Jyp strolled along the road, only stopping for a moment to peer in the window of a shop to see if he was being followed. Waiting for the man to pretend to bend down and do up his shoelaces, Jyp grabbed the opportunity and jumped on a bus as it slowed on the next corner, leaving his pursuer desperately waving for a taxi.

At the next stop, seeing the coast was clear, Jyp jumped off again and made for the nearest telephone kiosk. Turning up his collar, Jyp rang home, praying that his mother would be there and not out at one of her Bridge parties.

'Hello, who's that?' He caught her in the middle of a yawn, 'Is that you, dear. I'm so glad you rang. Where are you?'

'Never mind that, Ma. Has anyone been asking for me?'

'It's funny you should ask that, dear. I thought it was that friend of yours when you rang just now – what was her name, yes, that nice Patience – always talking about you, she is.'

The telephone shook in his hands. 'You didn't tell her where I was?'

There was a wondering laugh at the other end. 'I said I thought you were at the office, silly boy, where you always are. She was terribly worried – hasn't seen you all day.'

'Listen, don't tell her I've rung, whatever you do,' he said urgently. 'I'm coming home, but not a word to anyone. Promise?'

'Of course, silly. Oh, and she left a message, something about some figures she was after – deaths and that sort of thing. Said you'd understand.'

Jyp shuddered. 'They'll be mine soon, at this rate. Listen, Ma, leave the back door open so nobody sees me coming home. Can't explain now, I've got to get away for a few days – tell you all about it when I see you. Meanwhile, not a word to anyone.'

'You're not in trouble, are you dear?'

'No, no, nothing like that.' He glanced around nervously. 'I've got a new job – it's all hush-hush.'

'Nothing dangerous, is it – not like that 'wall of death' ride you were telling me about?'

Jyp lowered his voice. 'No, it's security, can't say any more now.'

'Ooh, er – wait till I tell your father, he'll want to know all about it.'

Holding back an inward scream, Jyp nearly dropped the phone. 'No, no, whatever you do – don't tell Dad. It'll be all around the British Legion before I get there. Listen, Ma,' he gulped, 'just throw a few things in a bag, you know, usual office clobber - pants and vests and a shirt just to keep me going. I'll be back as soon as I can to pick them up.'

'I know, I'll put that new suit of yours in – you know the one you were going to wear at that fancy dress party. It looked awfully smart – everyone was talking about it, I remember.'

'Not that one! Jyp shuddered. 'I never lived that down.'

'But Jyp...' At the sound of tapping on the window, Jyp was alarmed to see a small queue developing outside.

'Can't stop now, Ma, there's people waiting - see you later.'

'Oh dear, I forgot to tell you, love, we had an accident with the washing machine yesterday. The things came out all sorts of funny colours.'

'Doesn't matter, Ma - just find anything.'

'I know,' his mother persisted, 'I've still got those Mickey Mouse pants you wore on that Disneyland outing – you know the ones that squeaked when you sat down. Awfully funny that was – kept Dad in stitches for weeks.'

Jyp had had enough. 'Must go, Ma – bye.' He hastily slammed the phone down and swung round, half expecting to see his pursuer outside, waiting to pounce. Instead, it was an irate lady pointing at her watch. With a muttered apology, he escaped past her and the gathering queue and hurried down the road, pulling his collar up and making for the nearest station.

Chapter Five

The Right Kind of Person

Easing himself quietly through the back door in the hope of collecting his bag without being seen, Jyp had not allowed for the unforeseen obstacle to his plans – Rosy, the cat. Catching sight of the bag his mother had ready, he made a beeline for it. No sooner had he started to lift the heavily laden bag off the table and turned to make his getaway, than the catastrophe occurred. At that point, the cat decided to welcome him home by winding herself around his ankle, with unfortunate consequences.

The resulting crash, as he reached out for support and only succeeded in pulling down a row of saucepans off the nearby shelf - one that at any other time might have been mistaken for a plane passing overhead - was enough to alert his mother who was dozing in the front room, awaiting his return.

'Hello? Is that you, dear?'

Picking himself up with difficulty and removing the tea strainer from his hair he called out hastily, 'Just off, Ma, can't stop.' He tried to pick up his bag and staggered a few steps before coming to a halt.

'It's no good, I can't manage this lot,' he complained, as he started pulling out some of the items. 'Ma, what the devil am I going to do with this - I'm not going mountain climbing? I mean to say,' he appealed, holding up a hooded suit in disbelief.

'Don't you believe it, you never know when you might need it, dear,' she said, appearing in the doorway. 'You might get a chill, and then where would you be.'

'More likely get a heart attack carrying this lot.' Despite her protests, he picked through the bag and selected some of the more essential items, dumping the rest on the table. 'There, that's all I need. Right I'm off,' and he made for the door.

'Wait! You can't go off just like that,' she protested. 'Where are you staying – how am I going to get in touch with you?'

'Ah,' he halted, undecided. 'I'll put up somewhere, don't worry. I'll let you know.'

'I know, why didn't I think of it before?' she beamed. 'What about your Auntie Cis?'

'What about her?' he asked weakly, his hand on the door.

'She's always offering to have us stay with her if we ever get stuck – why, she'd love to have you. Wait, I'll give her a ring.'

'Do I have to?'

'Not another word. I can't have you wandering halfway around the countryside looking for lodgings, dear. She'll never forgive us,' she scolded as she busily dialled her sister. 'Hello? Is that you, Cis? Can you put Jyp up for a few days?' and proceeded to settle down for a long and cosy chat.

'Mother,' he shifted his feet impatiently.

'Here you are, dear,' she handed over the phone. 'Auntie Cis wants to let you know how to get there.'

'Oh, all right,' he grumbled and putting the bag down reluctantly took the receiver from her. 'Hello, Aunt Cis? Jyp here.'

While he was engaged, his mother tiptoed across the room and picked up what she decided would be essential items, tucking them back in his bag with a smile of triumph. 'There, that's better.'

It was not until much later that afternoon that Jyp wearily paused in front of a terraced row of houses near Plumpton Green and put his bag down with a sigh of relief. 'Ah, this must be it.' As he consulted the scribbled note his mother had given him to make sure, the door flew open and a suitcase flew out, followed by a sprawling body collapsing at his feet. As he glanced up, an indignant lady appeared at the top of the steps brandishing a broom shouting, 'And don't you come back either!'

As the man got to his feet sheepishly and slunk off, Jyp recognised the lady in question to be his Aunt Cicely.

'Hi – Aunt Cis,' he called out nervously. 'It's me – Jefferson!'

His aunt came down the steps still wearing her belligerent look. Fearing a sudden assault, Jyp stepped back uncertainly as she raised her arms.

'Is that Jyp?'

Relieved to see that she no was longer wielding her broom, Jeff allowed himself to be gathered into her arms and given a smacking great kiss. 'Come here and say hello to your poor old Auntie. Why, I haven't seen you for ages. I hear you're looking for a room for a few days – you're more than welcome, dear.'

'Are you sure it's not too much trouble?' he asked, nodding at the departing figure.

'Oh him!' she snorted. 'Hasn't paid his rent for months and expects me to provide free meals on tap. Anyone would think this is liberty hall,' she added ruefully. 'I've got my overheads to think of.'

'Does that mean you've got room for one more?' he asked hopefully.

'I wouldn't dream of charging you – why you're family! Come on in – why hello, Dave.'

Her remark was addressed to a policeman who appeared behind them, touching his helmet. 'Morning Mrs Green. Hear you're having trouble with a tenant,' giving Jyp a sideways glance of appraisal.

Aunt Cicely beamed. 'This my nephew, Jefferson, Dave. Jyp, say hello to my friend Dave – I should say Sergeant Ferris.' Jyp nodded politely. Explaining Jyp's presence, Aunt Cis went on, 'He's staying with me for a few days. No, that other one has gone, thank goodness. Owed me rent from way back – good riddance, I say.'

'Ah, well I'll be on my way, ma'am. Just checking.' He hesitated. 'A word in your ear, if I may. Between you and me, I've got a new boss breathing down my neck, so don't go chasing too many more tenants around with that broom of yours for a lark, 'cause he's bound to blame me about it. He's just looking for an excuse to pull me up.'

'And who's that when he's at home, Dave?'

Taking a quick look behind him, Sergeant Ferris whispered, 'Grooch.'

'I'm sorry, it get's me sometimes like that, as well. I'll have to let you have my latest spot of medicine. Works wonders.'

'No, that's his name. Inspector Grooch.'

Aunt Cis choked on a laugh. 'You're joking. Well, sounds as if it suits him. Bye, Dave.'

'He's a good sort, is Dave.' She gave him a cheerful wave of farewell. 'Now what am I thinking of – come in Jyp and I'll get you settled, and you can tell me all your news.'

Over a cup of tea, Jyp spoke in guarded tones about his new job and haltingly described himself as 'a kind of civil servant'. He spoke vaguely of security involved, then hesitated, wondering how to put it.

To his surprise, his Aunt tapped him playfully. 'You don't have to tell me – I know, you're working for that spy shop round the corner, aren't you.' Seeing his confusion, she explained, 'My cleaner, Elsie, works there on a Monday – you ought to hear some of the funny things going on there, she's always telling me about it.'

Taking pity on his confusion, she laughed. 'Don't worry – I know all about that line of business. I was in the same game myself at one time, so I know all about security.'

'Eh?'

Ignoring his startled reaction she got up briskly. 'Not actively, you understand, but enough to know what was going on.' Seeing his blank response, she continued lightly, 'We all have our own little secrets if you did but know. However, enough said, drink up and I'll show you your room. Don't forget,' she called over her shoulder, 'if you want to confide in me at any time, don't worry. It won't get beyond these four walls.'

As he dropped off to sleep, Jyp tried to take in the news about his aunt and couldn't help chuckling to himself, picturing the expression on his father's face if he ever found out.

He woke up early next morning after a sound sleep, eager to get started at his new job and relieved to have an ally close at hand in the event of an emergency. He studied his aunt covertly over breakfast, secretly impressed at her unexpected revelations, and intending to learn more about her mysterious past when an opportunity arose.

Unpacking his case after breakfast, he regarded the clothes dubiously, picking out the ones that looked the least garish. He dressed in them reluctantly, vowing to himself to go and get a decent suit as soon as he could afford it.

Because of the close proximity of his office he was able to present himself at the shop entrance well in time to start work precisely at nine o'clock.

When he entered the office Julie looked up from her desk with a warm smile. 'Ready for the school run?'

'What is that all about?' he asked anxiously. 'Nothing to do with children, is it?' Seeing her amused smile, he confessed. 'I was never any good at school – the teachers thought I was hopeless.'

Remembering his efforts at adding up, Julie smiled to herself. 'No, nothing like that. It's quite simple really. All you have to do is to leave a message in the phone box for an agent to pick up – it's just an exercise to get you used to the routine, if you get asked to do it.'

'Ah,' said Jyp cautiously. 'Sounds straightforward. When do I start?'

'When the Major gets in.' She leaned forward confidentially. 'We're not supposed to know this, but he's doing a round at the golf course at the moment. He'll be back soon. Ah, that sounds like him.'

Crash. The door banged open and the Major appeared looking flustered. 'Has anyone been asking for me?'

Despite being reassured, Major Fanshaw dropped his briefcase and hurried past calling over his shoulder. 'I'm in, if anyone wants to know – just hold on to them for a minute, I've got something important to do.'

'Right, that means half an hour practising his shots in his waste paper basket.' She got up resignedly. 'I suppose he wants me to do the honours. You wait here while I go and fetch the message, I don't know what he's done with it. It's around here somewhere...oh blow, that's the phone again. Do me a favour will you? Have a look, will you, while I'm answering the phone? It should be in locker thirteen, the same as our office number. He's probably dropped it down there somewhere. He's so absentminded these days... Hello? Modern Sportswear Ltd. Who's that?'

As she bent over the desk to listen, Jyp obediently searched along the lockers, counting as he went and scratching at his head as he arrived at different numbers every time until he accidentally kicked the briefcase, spilling out a package among the contents. Jyp picked it up and waved to Julie, mouthing, 'Got it!'

Holding a hand over the handset, Julie looked up and smiled briefly. 'It's the telephone box up the road – you can't miss it. Just leave it inside and someone will pick it up – good luck.'

Setting off down the road, Jyp espied the phone booth and after checking the coast was clear, he dropped the package inside and was just withdrawing when a hand fell on his shoulder and turning he came face to face with Dave, the friendly sergeant.

'Fancy meeting you again, sir.' He looked past Jyp at the phone booth. 'Is that yours?'

'No, no,' blurted Jyp instinctively. 'I – um...'

'Looks as if someone's left it in there by mistake. No, don't you bother, sir, I'll get it - that's what you pay your taxes for.'

'But,' Jyp began.

Just as he spoke a man came around the corner making for the phone box, and seeing the policeman began to turn around and make off.

'Wait,' called out Jyp automatically, 'you've forgotten the message,' and diving into the phone box grabbed hold of it and ran after him, thrusting it in his reluctant hands.

Uncertain what to do, the man decided to make a dash for it. Seeing the man escaping without an explanation, the sergeant called after him. 'Hi, wait a moment!'

Running slap into a couple coming round the corner the man in question started to panic, and whipping out a gun pointed it at them. 'Keep back!'

'Blimey!' gasped the sergeant. Drawing his whistle, he fumbled for his mobile.

Then everything seemed to happen at once. The young man who was coming towards them caught sight of the gun and taking advantage of the situation pushed his companion aside and made an awkward attempt to grab at the weapon.

'Hold him, sir,' shouted the sergeant. 'Don't let him get away.'

Seeing the game was up the gunman didn't wait to find out. Wriggling free, he dropped the package in his haste to get away and bolted back down the street.

Deprived of his suspect the sergeant turned his attention to what was left behind. 'Right,' he said standing back, 'let's see see what all the fuss was about.' He picked up the package and examined it. 'What have we got here?'He turned to Jyp. 'Give me a hand, will you, sir, there's something funny going on here.'

But Jyp was gone.

Back at the office the Major was getting increasingly restive. He turned to Julie, fuming. 'Where the devil has that man got to? It's only around the corner and he's been gone nearly half an hour! I could have finished a round of golf in that time. Well, I can't waste my time standing about here.' He checked his watch. 'I'm expecting an important call any moment, Julie. Put it through to my office and see that I'm not disturbed.'

'Very good, sir.'

However, the call when it came was not the one he had expected.

It produced a startled gasp from Julie and sent her hot foot to the Major's door where she disregarded the sign and knocked without ceremony.

After a few moments, the door opened abruptly and the furious face of Major Fanshaw appeared. 'I thought I told you,' he began, then seeing the expression on his secretary's face, snapped, 'Well, what is it?'

She swallowed. 'It's Special Branch, sir. They insist on having a word with you. Something about a package they've found.'

'Package? What package?'

'They say it was found in a telephone box - where Jefferson was sent on his school run.'

At the mention of Jyp, Major Fanshaw went purple. 'I knew he would get it wrong – the fool.' A horrible thought struck him. 'You did give him the right one, didn't you – the one I left in the locker? I don't believe it - out of my way!' He stumbled passed her and caught sight of his empty briefcase on the floor.

'You imbecile! You didn't?'

Just then, a head poked around the door and Reg looked in apologetically. 'There's a gentleman anxious to see you, sir. Says he's from Special Branch.'

There are some experts around who will tell you that it is not possible to leave an office at the speed Major Fanshaw-Smythe achieved at that precise moment. But they were wrong. One moment he was there and that next he was gone, accompanied by a whirring noise. As Julie remarked later in awe, 'He didn't even stop to pick up his golf clubs.'

* * *

Elsewhere in the heart of Whitehall, two senior officials were discussing the implications of the security disaster.

'Morning, Binky.'

'Morning, Trevor. Have you heard the ghastly news?'

'Yes, awful – can't bear to think about it.'

'I never thought it would come to this.'

'Nor did I. When I heard, I could hardly take it in. What's the latest?'

'Brace yourself old man, you might need a snifter.'

Trevor gulped. 'Go on then.'

'England all out for 23 runs.'

'Can't believe it.'

'They'll never live it down.'

'Don't suppose they will.'

'Ah well, I suppose we must carry on, and all that. Chin up, chest out.'

'I don't suppose there could be anything worse than that happening, Binky.'

'Only a spot of trouble down in the sticks, I hear – you know the one we were talking about yesterday. Just come through on the wire. That chap Fanshaw's done a bunk.'

'Oh him. What's he been up to?'

'Only tried to flog details of one of our nuclear sites in exchange for his green fees.'

'That doesn't surprise me. Never did trust him anyway.'

'Steady on, old man. He was your cousin after all.'

'I know, that's what makes it worse.'

'And he was one of us. You know, Eton and Guards background, and all that stuff. What did you have against him?'

'He tried to win our local golf tournament after I saw him pick up the ball when nobody was watching and drop it in the bally hole.'

'Well, he won't get much chance of playing golf where he's going – Siberia, I hear. Not many greens there.'

After a few desultory exchanges, Trevor scratched his head. 'Yes, that's all very well, but what do we do now. What about the papers - what are we going to tell them?'

'Oh, we'll think of something. You know, suffering from overwork. Given extended leave to get over it, usual sort of thing. Our PR man will see to that.'

'Yes, but who will we pick to replace him?'

'Ah well, I suppose it will have to be old pieface, you know, his deputy, what's his name - old Grimshaw, that's right. I should know, he's my wife's brother. Nothing to write home about – face like a horse, but I suppose he'll have to do until anything else turns up.'

'Wasn't he some sort of fitness instructor from some school or other, I seem to remember?'

'Yes, don't get him on that subject, whatever you do. He'll have you doing hand springs and a quick sprint around the block, before you know it – and that's only starters.'

'Good. Well, I'm glad we've sorted that out, Binky.'

'Exactly. So I'll leave it to you, Trevor, to fix things up.'

'No trouble. I'd better get cracking, otherwise that outfit down there will be wondering what's going on, especially that new recruit we've got.'

'My word, he soon rumbled old Fanshaw, didn't he. We'll have to keep an eye on him – promising material there. What's his name, Jyp or something? Sounds like that horse I lost a packet on at Ascot the other day. What's his background?'

'What d'you mean, Binky old chap?'

'You know – is he one of us? Public school and all that rot?'

'Far as I can make out, he went to that funny place they all speak about - you know, Watlington County Grammar.'

'Not the one where someone tried to flog London Bridge to the Yanks?'

'None other. Tell you what, I wonder what our new recruit will make of old Grimshaw – sounds a bit of a tartar.'

'Wouldn't be surprised – scares the daylights out of our lot every year when he turns up as Father Christmas.'

'Love to be a fly on the wall when he takes over, what?'

'You took the words right out of my mouth, old chap.'

'Glad we had these few words, Binky. Good thing they've got us here to rely on, eh?'

'Exactly. Couldn't put it better myself. See you at the Club tonight, Trevor old man.'

Chapter Six

A Bit of a Tartar

Back at the office, the scene was a hive of activity. Police and unmarked cars were coming and going, with uniformed and plainclothes men piling out and disappearing inside at regular intervals, inviting curious glances from passers-by. It was not until later on that it started to quieten down again and the neighbourhood resumed its normal activity.

After a lengthy pause, a head peered out of the entrance to the local insurance office and Jyp appeared and, after freeing himself from the attentions of the insurance salesman inside, made his way cautiously back to the office.

As soon as put his foot inside, he was pounced on by Reg. 'Here, where've you been? All hell's been let loose.'

Feigning surprise, Jyp adopted his usual blank look of innocence. 'What's up?'

'Bluebottles all over the place and the boss has scarpered, that's what!'

'You're joking. I'd better go and see what's up then,' said Jyp, wondering to himself what on earth could have happened in the short time he had been away. 'Miss Julie still there?'

'Yes, poor luv. She's all of a tiswas.' He led the way and knocked at the door, 'Here you are then.' He glanced back apologetically. 'What am I doing? You should know the way by now,' Shrugging his shoulders, he added, 'Let's hope we'll all still be here tomorrow, after all this rumpus.'

'Don't worry, it won't be you who gets the chop - if anyone,' said Jyp moodily.

'Oh, do you know something that I don't?' Reg asked hopefully.

Fearful of what lay ahead, Jyp shook his head. 'I'll catch up with you later,' he answered hurriedly, as the door opened.

'Oh, hello.' Julie took a quick look at Reg and then back along the corridor before pulling Jyp in. 'See you, Reg.'

'Now then, Jyp,' she commanded, pushing him into a seat. 'What happened with the message?'

As he described his encounter with the spy and subsequent events, she laughed ironically. 'Some "school run"- what an introduction!'

'Why, what have I done?'

Seeing his look of bewilderment, Julie took pity on him. 'You've only been here five minutes, and on your very first day you managed to unmask one of the top double agents in the country and he turns out to be our very own, Major Fanshaw.'

'You're joking,' he said weakly. 'How come?'

She regarded him reprovingly. 'That package you picked up by mistake contained details of one of our,' looking around carefully, she lowered her voice, 'nuclear plants, and he was just going pass it over to the enemy for a whopping great sum so that he could pay his green fees.'

'No! What did he have to say about it?'

'Say? He didn't stay to explain – he was off like a shot. I've never seen him move so fast.'

Jyp sighed. 'So that's that. Another job gone up in smoke.' He got up heavily. 'Seems to be the story of my life. I'll say goodbye then - it's been nice knowing you, Julie.'

'Then you haven't heard?' Julie smiled, ready to break the news.

'Heard what?'

'Only that you're hero of the hour.'

'Eh?'

'According to Dave, our local Bobby, you not only exposed our chief as a double agent but you made sure the spy was caught red-handed with some of our top secrets. And,' she added triumphantly, 'he said you were too modest to wait around and you left him to take the credit – mind you, he could do with it, what with that Inspector of his breathing down his neck!'

'But,' protested Jyp, 'I didn't do anything.'

'That's not what Dave said. I shouldn't argue,' she added, seeing his look of bewilderment. 'It will go down on your record and give you a boost – not a bad start in our kind of game. Anyway, I must get on. We've been told to pack up and go home while the security people give the place the once-over.'

'How long will that take?'

'No idea, but we've got to be on parade at nine o'clock sharp tomorrow to meet our new boss, so don't be late.'

'Who's that?' asked Jyp, still at a loss.

'I gather he's our second in command.' She consulted her diary. 'Someone called Grimshaw, according to our records. Bit of a tartar, by all accounts.'

'That's all we need,' said Jyp with feeling.

'Cheer up, Jyp. You've got nothing to worry about after everything you've done.' Seeing the doubt linger in his face, she squeezed his arm reassuringly. 'Don't worry – everything's going to be fine, you'll see. We'll back you up.'

* * *

Listening to his recital after he got back to his lodgings, Aunt Cis pursed her lips thoughtfully.

'Grimshaw – funny, that rings a bell. I'm sure I've come across that name somewhere before.'

'I'd be very grateful if you could find out, Auntie Cis – it might be of help. I certainly need it.'

His aunt regarded him reassuringly. 'I know you have to tread a bit carefully, seeing that you've only just started there, but you know the trouble with you, Jyp, is that you're not very assertive. You need to stand up for yourself more. Take it from me, you're only storing up trouble for yourself otherwise. In this game, you'll find that other people will take advantage of you given half the chance. I should know all about it,' she added ruefully, 'in my time, being a woman was ten times worse.'

'Tell me something,' agreed Jyp moodily. 'If only I could.'

'Well, don't take it too seriously, otherwise that young lady of yours won't think much of you.'

Jyp coloured. 'I don't know that she does anyway,' he said wistfully.

His aunt got up briskly. 'Well she won't if you turn up looking like that – I must run your things through the washing machine and make sure you look spick and span for when you meet this new boss of yours – Grimshaw, did you say?'

'Yes, if you would, Aunt Cis. I don't want to give him the wrong impression. I wonder what he's like - I expect they'll send someone steady and reliable this time, to calm things down. They don't want a repeat of the last one.' He shuddered at the thought.

* * *

Despite his note of hopeful optimism, he found he was wrong on both counts when he was ushered into Grimshaw's office the next morning. The man who bounded up to greet him looked so full of energy he gave the impression of a firecracker about to go off.

'Hello. My name's Ernest Grimshaw, and I'm your new boss,' he boomed, pumping Jyp's hand. 'And who are you?'

'Jefferson Patbottom... er, sir.'

'Never mind, you can't help that. We all have our cross to bear. Now where was I?' he said, slowing his voice down to a series of barks. 'I've been asked to take over and put a bit of life into the works. A healthy office is a happy office, eh?' He broke off as Julie entered with a tray of tea. 'Oh thank you, my dear, put it down there, will you,' pointing to a nearby table. 'Well sit down, Jefferson, we don't stand on ceremony here.' He motioned to a seat and Jyp obeyed.

Immediately he did so, there was a loud squeak and Jyp realised with horror that his aunt had put out his joke pants to wear by mistake. He jumped to his feet in agitation and upset the table with the drinks on. 'Oops, sorry.' He dabbed at the dripping mess ineffectually, making it worse.

'Never mind that. Sit down, man. I'll get Julie to clear it up. Now, down to business.'

'I'll stand, if you don't mind,' excused Jyp hastily. 'Touch of cramp.'

'Sounds as if you need a bit of exercise, my lad. Oh, for Heavens sake, sit down. I can't talk to you like that.'

Jyp gingerly sat on the edge of the seat, waiting for a noise but nothing happened, so he relaxed a little and managed to set it off again.

'That does it, can't have you going around making noises like that – you'll upset Julie. On your feet, Jefferson, this calls for immediate action.' He got out his watch. 'Running on the spot, starting now!'

'But I don't need these exercises,' panted Jyp as he tried to keep up. 'You don't understand - it's these pants of mine.'

'Yes, I know, very irregular, I'm not deaf. You should see your doctor and get some medicine for it. Whatever it is, we need to clean out your system. Now, take a deep breath and start again, and if you must pant, see how I do it.'

Trying to explain and watching his boss at the same time proved too much of an effort, with the result that Jyp lost his balance and fell back on his seat yet again.

'Dear me, this will never do.' Grimshaw tut-tutted at the squeaks and rang a bell. When Julie appeared, he coughed, 'Jefferson and I are going out for a short while. We have important...ahem...things to discuss. Better in the open, where nobody can overhear them, eh, Jefferson?'

'Yes, sir,' agreed Jyp gratefully.

'Right then, carry on, Julie. If you could clear away the tea things – there seems to be some sort of upset.'

'Don't worry, I'll see to it.' She flashed a look of encouragement as Jyp tiptoed around the shattered cups. As he followed Grimshaw out he whispered to her hoarsely, 'Tell Reg to get me some pants!'

'Some what?'

'Some pants – I've got the wrong ones on!'

'Come along, Jefferson,' commanded Grimshaw impatiently from the doorway.

'Coming, sir,' Jyp called out. To Julie, 'Never mind – I'll explain later.' He hurried out, leaving Julie with an astonished look on her face.

* * *

Outside, Grimshaw waved a hand and set off at a fast pace. Looking back, he barked, 'Come along, come along, Jefferson. No time for slacking, we've got to get you fit. Follow me.'

Jyp hobbled along doing his best to avoid setting off his joke pants as he tried to keep up.

As they passed the newspaper shop Grimshaw slowed to read the placard outside and seeing the heading 'SPY LATEST' broke off and hurried in to pick up a newspaper while Jyp, taking advantage of the respite, leaned against the doorway, panting.

Before he had a chance to get his breath back Grimshaw emerged again waving the newspaper in front of him, snapping, 'We've got to get back – this needs looking into.'

Heaving a sigh of gratitude Jyp wheeled around and followed at a more leisurely pace, relieved that the exercise was over.

* * *

Back in the office, Grimshaw left him and disappeared into his office. Seizing the opportunity, Jyp leaned across the receptionist's desk asked Julie anxiously, 'Did Reg get those…um…things I asked for?'

Glancing up from a pile of papers a slightly harassed Julie replied distractedly, 'What things?'

'You know, my, um, pa…underwear.'

'Is that what you were trying to tell me?'

'Yes, of course,' he said feeling embarrassed. 'Well?'

'I passed on your message, such as it was, Jyp,' she answered briefly, looking up. 'You'd better ask him yourself. I'm rather busy just now with all this.' She waved a hand expressively.

'Ok, never mind.' He tried to twist himself into a more comfortable position and finally gave up.

'What was it you were trying to tell me?' Julie wanted to know as she pushed the papers aside later, but Jyp had gone.

'Pants?' repeated Reg disbelieving, when Jyp tracked him down. 'You're having me on. What's up with yours?'

Jyp told him tersely in a few words.

'Oooh, she didn't.' Reg giggled. 'You're kidding. No,' he changed his mind as Jyp sat down, dejected, and set it off again, 'I see what you mean. Look, I tell you what, you swap with me and I'll slip out and get something as soon as the rush dies down. Half a mo.'

And with that he disappeared into a recess and shortly afterwards an arm waved in the distance, dangling a tiny pair of briefs. 'Here, borrow mine for the time being. You can change in here.'

Jyp did as he was told, and peering out furtively took a few steps before his face creased in agony. 'I can't wear these, they're too tight – they're torture!'

'Sorry, Jyp, it's all I've got.' Reg's voice floated across from the other side of the shop. 'You'll have to wait until lunchtime. Here, these pants of yours don't half make a funny noise.'

Jyp walked back awkwardly to the office, keeping his steps as short as possible to ease the friction, but his odd behaviour was noticed directly Julie caught sight of him.

'Are you all right?'

'I'm fine – just fine,' Jyp managed with a painful smile. 'Thank goodness the route march is finished today.' He consulted his watch. 'It's nearly lunch time. I'll just nip out and see if I can get some more, um, something to help. There's bound to be a shop around here somewhere.'

But he was wrong again. To his horror, all the shops he encountered had a sign up reminding him that it was early closing. In desperation he made for his lodgings, knowing thankfully that he had a change of underwear there. But when he got there, he found his aunt was out and the front door closed, and remembered that today was her Bridge party day.

Frustrated, he staggered back to the office and to crown it all, he found that Julie had already gone to lunch, tired of waiting for him. He was reduced to hobbling to the nearest snack bar counter down a side street where he was forced to eat a ham roll standing up.

When he returned to the office, Julie was anxious to hear where he had been. 'What happened to you? I nearly missed my lunch waiting for you?'

'I, er, had to go to the shops.'

'But it's early closing today – didn't you know?'

He tried to ease his cramped conditions, pretending to search for something in his pocket. 'I do now, drat it.'

'Well anyway, you've come back just in time to help me.' She waved her hands at a mounting pile of typed letters. 'I've got all this lot to get posted – can you give me a hand?'

'Of course,' he agreed quickly, anxious to redeem himself after keeping her waiting, 'what can I do?'

'You can put some of this lot into envelopes. The big white chief wants to get it all into the post this afternoon. He keeps churning them out faster than I can handle them. I can't keep up with it. I ask you, what am I supposed to do?'

Putting his own problems aside for a moment, Jyp scratched his head. Then remembering Reg's offer to help, he jumped at the opportunity to serve his idol. 'Leave it to me – I'll have a word with Reg. I'm sure we can shift this lot between us.'

Storing up her look of gratitude, Jyp went in search of Reg, finding him just letting down the blinds before closing up.

'Coo, you caught me just as I was buzzing off. Do what? As long as it don't take too long. I must get these pants of yours changed – they don't half make some funny noises.'

'It won't take five minutes,' Jyp assured him heartily, dismissing the thought of the hundreds of letters waiting to be dealt with.

'Oh, all right then, 'alf a mo while I shut the shop up.' Satisfied at last, he followed Jyp back into the office and blinked at the avalanche that awaited. 'Blimey, five minutes, did you say?'

'Thank you so much,' Julie flung them a warm greeting. 'As soon as I get this lot finished, I'll come and give you a hand.'

Watching them go to work standing up, awkwardly stuffing envelopes, she pointed to a table behind them. 'Why don't you sit down over there, you'll find it much easier.'

'No, I'm quite all right,' Jyp winced as he shifted his position. 'I prefer to stand, thanks all the same.'

'What about you, Reg?' pressed Julie. 'You must be awfully tired after serving in the shop all morning.'

Reg looked longingly at a chair, then shook his head regretfully. 'I'm fine.' Then unable to resist the opportunity at having a dig. 'Just panting to get this done, eh Jyp?' he added slyly.

'We're just dressed for the part,' agreed Jyp manfully, tugging at his trousers.

Much later, as the last letter was folded and sealed in the envelope with a weary flourish, Reg glanced at his watch. 'Blimey, don't say we're finished, I don't believe it.'

Jyp straightened his back and tried moving a leg back and forwards to see if there was any life left in it. 'I hope so. That seems to be the lot,' he said cautiously, half expecting the door to open, signalling the arrival of another batch.

'Well, we'd better get this lot off,' Jyp decided at last, testing the weight of the sack containing the envelopes. They looked at each other hopefully, waiting for someone else to make an offer.

Seeing their predicament, Julie announced with regret. 'Sorry, I can't help – I've still got a hundred and one things to clear up. How about you, Reg - can you manage to get this lot to the post?'

Heaving a sigh, Reg picked up the sack with a struggle and staggered out, calling over his shoulder, 'Leave it to me – I'll see to it. I'll be glad to get home and sit down again, eh Jyp?'

Before Jyp could answer, they heard the office door open and Julie groaned. 'Not another lot, I hope.'

Instead of a further batch, it was Grimshaw himself who strode out and bore down on them. 'Ah, there you are, Jefferson. Where were we?'

'You were checking up on that newspaper headline,' offered Jyp quickly, hoping to stave off any more demands for typing as he gamely marshalled his scattered thoughts, while trying to remember details of their last encounter.

Grimshaw frowned dismissively. 'It was just one of those silly rumours floating around. I soon told the editor what to do with it and had it squashed.' His voice rose indignantly. 'I told him to come to me next time he has a report like that – he had the nerve to make out we had no effective border control. I ask you, what does he think we're here for?'

'You didn't tell him?' squeaked Julie before she could stop herself.

Luckily, Grimshaw was too full of his own concerns to notice. 'Of course not, they don't call us "the silent service" for nothing. However, I've been thinking. Now that this has come up, I'm afraid this means we will have to postpone our beneficial exercise programme for the time being, Jefferson. No,' he raised a hand, missing the overwhelming expression of relief on Jyp's face, 'I know this will upset you but I'm afraid there are other more important issues that have to come first.'

'Not at all,' gulped Jyp manfully. 'I'll make out.'

'Don't think I haven't forgotten,' Grimshaw unbent. 'We will get back to it as soon as I can. I know how much you miss it.'

'Thank you, sir.'

In the background, Julie repressed a grin.

'Meanwhile, with all this work coming in, I can see we will have to make some changes around here, to lessen the load on the office.'

At his words, Julie brightened.

'I don't want this present system continuing any longer – I can see it is too much to expect with our existing level of staff. It's not fair to either of you.'

'Does that mean I get an assistant?' asked Julie hopefully.

'I have a much better plan than that,'answered Grimshaw, slapping Jyp on the back. 'After all those reports of this young man's sterling work, I have decided to reward him by giving him more responsibility. I have arranged for the stationery room to be made available as his office and I have appointed a Miss Plackett to be his secretary.' He glanced at his wrist watch, 'Ah, that must be her now. Excuse me while I explain the situation to her.'

His departure left a stunned silence that was broken by Julie. 'Congratulations, Jyp,' I'm so glad for you.' Musing, 'Mind you, I could do with some help myself.' She waved a hand at the remaining pile of dictation next to her. Noticing his apparent lack of enthusiasm, she exclaimed, 'You don't seem very excited about it?'

Jyp turned to her exasperatedly. 'I can't think about it while I've got these blessed...'

Full of embarrassment, he was about to make a full confession when the door opened and Grimshaw appeared and introduced them to an attractive young lady who Reg described later as "a corker".

Noting their open mouths Grimshaw broke the awkward gap, 'Here you are, Jefferson, this is your new secretary, Miss Gladys Plackett. I think I've got that right, young lady?'

'Charmed, I'm sure.' The young lady in question beamed in modest confusion, fluttering her eyes at Jyp.

Before anyone could think of what to say next, Grimshaw made an expansive gesture.

'To celebrate the new arrangements, I have decided that we get to know each other more informally. With this in mind, I have booked a table at a charming hostelry that someone I know has recommended.' He looked at his watch and laughed jovially, 'Why, bless my soul, I see we're due there in ten minutes. We'd better put a move on, or we'll get a bad name with the chef. Can't have that, can we? You lead the way, Miss Diamond, as you know the neighbourhood.'

Bewildered, Julie reminded him, 'Where is it, sir?'

'Oh, good heavens, I haven't mentioned, have it? I believe they call it, "The Happy Warrior".'

'Oh goodness, that dump.' Julie reacted without thinking. 'I mean,' she tried to be tactful, 'it has a certain reputation for... a rather different kind of entertainment, I understand. I'm sure it will do splendidly,' she added hastily.

'Well, it's up to us to try it out, so come along we don't want to be late.'

Julie shot a quick apologetic look at Jyp and led the way.

Whatever misgivings Julie had expressed turned out to be well justified. The interior of hostelry in question wore a forlorn look and gave the impression that it had just recovered from a police raid and was doing its best to pull itself together, without much success.

Despite that, Grimshaw seemed determined to make the most of the occasion and spent most of his time exchanging greetings with a number of seedy looking strangers passing their table who seemed to know him very well. He appeared so engrossed that Julie, remembering that she should be deputising as hostess, started nodding her head meaningly at Jyp then at Gladys as the band struck up and various couples started getting up to dance.

Appalled at the idea of trying to move around the floor handicapped by Reg's pants, Jyp did his best to ignore her signals until Julie leaned across the table and hissed, 'Ask her, you idiot!'

Swallowing, Jyp got up awkwardly and make some polite gestures, groaning inwardly at the effort involved. Delighted to be asked, Gladys got up eagerly, more than willing to join the dancers. It became immediately obvious to her that she had made a big mistake as Jyp took hold of her clumsily and winced as the pants began to bite in the most unexpected places.

Misinterpreting his actions, Gladys snuggled up closer and simpered, 'There, is that better? I wasn't being very friendly, was I?'

Feeling hampered by her clinging embrace, he cast an appealing glance for help in Julie's direction but only received a distant look in return.

Unable to ignore his peculiar method of dancing, his partner gave a coy look of enquiry as he trod on her foot yet again. 'Is there anything wrong?'

Grasping eagerly at the opportunity, Jyp put on a brave face, 'Sorry, it's my gammy leg.'

'Oh,' she managed to sound disappointed as several couples cannoned into them. 'Just as we were getting to know each other. Perhaps we should sit this out, then.'

Relieved, he led her back to the table only to face Julie's unspoken criticism.

'Such a divine dancer,' Gladys trilled bravely, slipping her feet out of her shoes to ease the aches.

'I'm so glad you're enjoying it,' replied Julie sweetly, attempting to keep a note of reproof out of her voice.

There was a sudden pause as Jyp tried to think of a safer topic. Before he could come up with anything, Grimshaw appeared again and noting the restrained atmosphere announced jovially, 'I say, this is jolly, I've had a brilliant time – met all sorts of new friends. Nobody dancing? Come now, what about you, Miss Diamond. Care for a turn?'

'Not just now,' Julie refused politely, waiting to hear what Jyp had been up to. 'Perhaps a little later.'

'Oh,' remarked Grimshaw, not to be outdone. 'What about you, Miss Plackett?'

Unable to refuse an implied command, Gladys slipped her feet back into her battered shoes and smiled brightly. 'Why, I'd love to.'

Directly they were out of earshot, Julie couldn't wait. In the short time they had got to know each other she was beginning to feel more than just a chum to Jyp and couldn't hide a twinge of jealousy. 'What were you up to out there? You were making a right spectacle of yourself.'

'I...er,' he was about to repeat his excuse about a gammy leg when her expression told him this was out of the question, and he decided to come clean. As he began to unburden himself, her look of stern disapproval began to melt and a note of hysteria crept into her voice and she began to giggle so loudly that nearby dancers started edging closer hoping to pick up the thread of their conversation in order to relieve the tedium of their depressing surroundings.

'Why on earth didn't you tell me before?' she gasped at last, between snorts. 'You poor thing, you must be suffering,' she nearly said "agonies" but substituted, 'feeling awful?'

Squirming at the thought, Jyp tried to defend himself. 'It's not something I could talk about.'

'You idiot,' she sighed, wiping the tears from her eyes. 'Surely you know by now I'd understand?' She stopped, aware of a tender feeling engulfing her, utterly unlike her previous relationship when she had regarded herself more as a sister. From now on she felt she could no longer think of him just as a friend, but there was something else that was welling up inside her, that somehow made him a little more special than any man had before. Putting her feelings aside with an effort, she tried to concentrate on the practicalities. 'Well, what are you going to do about it?'

He heaved a sigh. 'It's early closing, so I suppose I'll have to wait until I get home and change.'

'You can't possibly wait till then,' Julie decided firmly. 'Here,' she fished a pair of miniature scissors out of her handbag. 'Why don't you use these – I find them jolly useful.'

He took them gingerly. 'What am I supposed to do with these?'

She sighed. 'Go and cut yourself loose, of course. There's a Gents over there,' she indicated. 'I can't do it for you – they don't allow ladies in there,' she grinned impishly.

'Thanks, I never thought I'd have to do this. Poor old Reg, he quite fancied these.'

'He won't mind, it's all for a good cause. Go on.'

'You sure you'll be all right?' He hesitated, glancing at the noisy revelry going on around them.

'Course I will,' she urged. 'Don't worry, the others will be back soon.'

But she was wrong. As soon as he freed himself from the tattered remains with a sigh of bliss and stepped out into the dance hall again he was met by a deserted floor.

The next moment, a heavy hand descended on his shoulder and an authoritative voice announced in his ear with satisfaction, 'You're nicked.'

Chapter Seven

Raining Banknotes

As he was led into the police station the desk sergeant looked up, harassed, and he recognised his old friend Dave. 'Not you as well, sir?' Let's have your name then.'

'Jefferson Patbottom.'

'Ask a silly question. Right, how do you spell that?' He proceeded to write it down laboriously. 'P-a-t-b-o-t-t-o-m. Address? Oh, I know that, of course. Right, sir, the constable will take you to our interview room for the usual search procedure.' Reacting to the questioning look on Jyp's face, he explained. 'It's only routine, sir. We have to do the same for anyone caught in that place. No wonder they call it "The Happy Warrior" – not surprising, they're always stoned out of their mind after the stuff they serve there. Right,' he motioned to the constable, 'take this gentleman to join the others. You'll find your lot already down there. And if I might make a suggestion, sir, don't let them talk you into going there again.'

'Don't worry – I won't,' said Jyp with feeling, as he was led out.

Shaking his head, the Sergeant picked up a phone and said, 'Get me Mrs Green on the line, luv, will you?' As the call came through, he coughed apologetically. 'That you, Cis, I've got your lodger here. Can't explain now. You'd better come and pick him up.'

Inside, after submitting to a search, Jyp found the others clustered around a red faced Grimshaw who was waving his arms around furiously. 'How much longer am I to be kept waiting like this – it's intolerable. I demand to see the Chief Constable. Ah, it's you, Jefferson,' he calmed down. 'What's happening out there?'

'It appears that restaurant is well known to the police, sir,' Jyp offered apologetically.

'The constable tells me it's a well known drug centre.'

'Drug centre? Nonsense. Some of my best friends go there.'

Julie caught his eye in the background and nodded significantly.

As the words sank in, the constable popped his head around the door. 'The sergeant would like to see you now, sir. If you'll step this way.'

Bristling, Grimshaw stalked out, followed by the others, anxious not to be left behind.

At the desk, Jyp caught sight of his Aunt Cis and heaved a sigh of relief, mixed with embarrassment at being discovered in such a situation.

Marching up to the desk, Grimshaw thumped on it, breaking up a conversation the Sergeant was having with Jyp's aunt.

'On what charges are we being held, sergeant?' he demanded.

Straightening up, Sergeant Ferris regarded him mildly. 'Well now, sir, there is a question of you being on unlicensed premises and drinking intoxicating liquor. I could hold you over until the morning until the magistrate arrives.'

'Oh,' said Grimshaw calming down, 'I see, hrm, like that, eh?'

'There could be a small matter of a fine in cases like these.'

'Well, if that's all it means,' Grimshaw beamed, 'I don't think you'll find me ungenerous.

If I can make a small contribution to the Police funds, perhaps that will help?' He got out his wallet and slapped a fistful of notes on the desk in front of the astonished sergeant, eliciting a gasp from the others.

Mistaking the hushed silence as a signal that his offer was only an opening bid, Grimshaw dived into his pocket and threw a packet of notes on the counter. 'There, how about that, then?'

Coughing discreetly, the sergeant swept the notes into a container and shut the lid.

'I think that should more than adequately cover the costs, sir. In that case, I think we might regard the incident as closed. You are free to go.'

Drawing himself up importantly, Grimshaw announced, 'I should think so, too.' To the others, he rumbled, 'I hope you will keep details of this evening to yourself – it will be much better for all concerned in the circumstances.'

As Jyp followed them out, the sergeant leaned over and advised him confidentially, 'If I may offer a suggestion, sir, it is always wise to make sure you have a pair of undergarments on in that kind of establishment, it tends to send out the wrong kind of signal – especially to my Inspector.' He shuddered. 'Luckily, it's his day off.'

'Don't worry – I will,' promised Jyp fervently.

Outside, Julie drew Jyp aside. 'Well, what do you think of that?'

Thinking back over what had occurred, Jyp answered thoughtfully. 'I don't like to say it, but I think he's up to something, Julie. Who were all those unsavoury characters he met in the restaurant? They seemed very chummy – a bit too chummy, if you ask me.'

'Yes, and what about all those letters he's been sending out – asking if they've got a job for all those people he says he's cleared?'

Jyp pondered. 'If only we could find out what he's been up to – I wonder if there's anything in that office of his that would give us a clue?'

Julie grabbed his arm excitedly. 'I know, why don't we have a look and see for ourselves?'

'How do we do that when he's there all the time?'

'I don't mean tomorrow – what's wrong with tonight? I've got a key.'

'What, now?'

'No time like the present, before your landlady wants to know where you are.'

'Ok,' agreed Jyp wonderingly, infected by her enthusiasm. 'Let's go.'

As he followed her into the darkened office Jyp marvelled at her temerity in bearding the lion's den, and began to see her in a new light.

'Come on,' she urged while he hesitated for a moment outside Grimshaw's office. 'Hold the torch, while I try the key. Eureka!' she murmured as the door gave way. 'Now, we're getting somewhere.' She halted at his desk and gazed around. 'Where do we start?'

'Why don't you try his desk, while I check that filing cabinet?'

'Good thinking – we haven't got much time. I wonder what Dad would have thought about this?' she chortled. 'He's terribly upright about this sort of thing. He'd have a fit.'

'We haven't got time to go into the niceties,' whispered Jyp. 'Let's get cracking.'

'Right. Here, take a look at this!' Julie pulled out a drawer revealing a mass of bank notes, stacked in bundles.

'Wow!' He took one look and whistled. 'He's obviously got that lot out to pay someone – the question is – who?' He moved over to the filing cabinet and eased out a drawer. 'Let's have a decko.' After a few minutes delving he turned to Julie. 'Looks like a cross section of industry here with a list of all the insiders he's been in touch with. And he's only been here five minutes. He must have been doing this for months, long before he came here. And this proves it - look!' He pulled out another drawer. 'Here's a list of the people he's trying to get cleared for security – that's where all the money must be coming from…bribery!'

They looked at each other.

Julie struck a practical note. 'How are we going to prove it?'

Recalling his last conversation with his aunt, Jyp had a sudden idea. 'Let's take some samples of each of the lists and I'll show them to Aunt Cis – she tells me she was involved in security at one time – she might know what to do. She even might remember coming across our sainted boss – she said the name was familiar.'

'Ok,' agreed Julie, relieved they were getting somewhere at last. 'You check with your Auntie Cis, and let me know in the morning.'

Mention of his aunt made Jyp start guiltily. 'I'd better get back, I expect she'll be wondering where I've got to.'

'And I must get back – bye Jyp. Thanks for your help.' She touched his arm in gratitude.

The feel of her warm hand made Jyp jump and instinctively he reached out to find her. The next minute she was in his arms and he found himself kissing her.

Breaking off with a gasp, Julie decided she quite liked the experience. 'I'd better go now, she said breathlessly. 'See you tomorrow,' and shooed him out before locking the door behind them.

Jyp wandered back to his lodgings in a blissful daze, reliving every moment of their embrace. He was in such a state that his aunt commented on it when he appeared. 'Wake up Jyp, you look as if you've run into a lamppost.'

'She let me kiss her,' was his dreamy response.

'Well, don't go into the office like that – they'll think you're drunk,' was her immediate reaction. 'I should sit down and take the weight off your feet. Anyway, what's all this about – "she let me"?' she demanded, harking back to his previous remark. 'That's not the sort of talk I expect any nephew of mine to use - are you a man or a mouse?'

'I don't care, Aunt Cis – she let me,' he repeated, sinking back blissfully on the sofa.

'Right, well we'll go into that later,'she dismissed the idea. 'What I want to talk about is that boss of yours – Grimshaw.'

'Grimshaw,' he repeated vaguely, still lost in a romantic cloud.

'Yes, Grimshaw. Listen, I told you I thought that name was familiar, didn't I?' Well, when I clapped eye on him, I knew I was right. I remember now, he was involved in some sort of scandal with a pupil of his at that school you went to – Watlington something or other.'

'County Grammar,' Jyp automatically finished, making an effort to show some interest.

'Well, it got to a stage where it was reported to the Head that he got a girl in trouble and he was fired. How about that? I knew there was something about that name.'

'Gosh.'

'I thought that would get your attention,'she replied with satisfaction. 'And what was all that about him splashing all that money about? You don't get that sort of money on civil service pay – at least you didn't when I was there.'

'Ah, you don't know the half of it, Auntie.' And he proceeded to bring her up to date on his recent discoveries at the office, handing over examples of their finds for her to see.

'That explains it.' she mused, examining the cards. 'I wonder what his game is? I should watch your step, if I were you, Jyp. If you're right, he could be making a mint out of letting in all kinds of villains. We need to prove it before we do anything.'

As he shifted his position awkwardly, she softened. 'I'm sorry about those pants of yours – I don't know what happened there.' She hid a smile. 'If you'll let me have them, I'll post them back to your ma to look after.'

He was about to hand over the tattered remnants when he suddenly remembered. 'Don't bother, Aunt. They're not mine anyway. I did a swap with someone in the office.'

'Oh,' she grinned, 'just as well. He won't be using those anymore, will he. Would you like me to put some ointment on the, um, sore places?'

'No, don't worry about that,' he said hastily. 'I'll see to it. I'll be off, then. Good night, Aunt Cis.'

'Right you are. Off you go, perhaps after a good night's sleep we can think up some way of sorting it out between us.'

* * *

In the morning with no clearer idea what to do, Jyp was initially more concerned with making sure he had a decent pair of pants to wear. Racking his brains, he went over the details in his mind about what they knew about Grimshaw and was about to leave for the office when it occurred to him.

'We don't know the name of this girl you mentioned, I suppose? You know, the one he got into trouble.'

'Let me see.' his aunt chewed her pen thoughtfully as she was finishing off a postcard to her sister. 'I believe her name was Maggie something or other. Leave it with me – I'll have a think about it.' Knowing her remarkable fund of memories, Jyp was content to leave it at that. 'By the way,' she called after him, 'do you want me to explain to your mother about what happened to your nice pair of pants?'

Jyp shuddered, knowing what was likely to happen if his dad heard about it. 'Don't even mention the word, Auntie. I'd never hear the last of it.'

But he was soon to discover that his aunt wasn't the only one who wanted to know.

Directly he got into the office Julie looked up and warned him, 'The old man wants to see you right away, Jyp. Something to do with your, um,' she looked around guardedly, 'you know, what you were wearing yesterday.'

Putting on an expression of innocence, Jyp knocked on the door. 'You wanted to see me, sir?'

'Ah yes, Jefferson, come in. Sit down, oh,' he broke off hurriedly, 'unless you find it more convenient to stand.'

Jyp obeyed, waiting to hear the reason for his summons.

Clearing his throat, Grimshaw fiddled with his papers. 'I understand from a report at the police station yesterday that you were not, um, carrying any illegal drugs, or anything like that, but more importantly that you were not wearing any, um, underwear – is that true?'

Relieved to hear that their previous search of the office had remained undetected, Jyp took heart and tried to dismiss the subject blithely. 'Yes, my aunt persuaded me to leave them off because of the hot weather. You see, she's one of these outdoor healthy types.'

Grimshaw cleared his throat again. 'Well, whatever the reason, your recent, hem, behaviour convinces me that we must get back to our regular routine of outdoor exercises again as a basis for a healthy life.'

Eager to avoid the subject of their break-in cropping up, Jyp quickly agreed. 'I'm ready,' he broke off inquiringly, 'as long as it's not interfering with anything you had in mind for our new secretary, Miss, er...'

Rising from his seat, Grimshaw coughed, 'I fear the experience yesterday proved to be too much for Miss Plackett and, hrm, I regret to say that after her experience at the police station, she has decided to seek employment elsewhere. Now,' reverting to his favourite topic, 'as I was saying, we must get back to that excellent exercise, commence with running on the spot. Are we ready, starting now.'

Jyp got to his feet reluctantly and followed suit, falling in behind Grimshaw as he led the way out of the office. Passing Julie he raised his eyebrows expressively and she tried not to grin, thankful that she was free from any more dictation for a brief period at least while they exercised around the office block.

But as subsequent events turned out, they were about to be brought to a halt by an unexpected note of high drama that neither of them were expecting.

Puffing into the straight, as their office entrance appeared in the distance for the second time that morning, Jyp was suddenly petrified by the sound of a familiar voice floating down from the top of a passing sightseeing bus.

'Yoohoo, Jyp!'

Jerked out of his weary grind, Jyp took one look and froze at the sight of the last person he ever expected to see again in his worst nightmare waving at him – Patience!

'Who was that?' Grimshaw looked back over his shoulder for an answer but Jyp had already passed him on the other side, running at full speed for the haven of the office as if his life depended on it.

Behind him there was a squeal of brakes and a lorry ploughed into the back of the tourist bus as the harassed driver tried to brake in answer to the insistent demands from the top deck.

Springing off the bus as it tried to avoid a head-on collision with another bus, Patience looked frantically up and down the street for a sight of her quarry. In her haste to renew the chase, Patience nearly knocked a man off his bicycle as he wobbled past.

'Which way did he go?' demanded Patience. 'I must find him!'

The man picked himself up groggily and was joined by the aggrieved bus driver wanting to know what she thought she was playing at.

'Oh, I haven't got time to argue with you.' Patience lost her temper. 'I'll look for myself.' And brushing aside the onlookers, she marched off along the street looking for signs of Jyp, followed by cries of 'What about my bus?' and 'wotcha done with me bike?'

Back at the office Julie was taken aback at the sudden appearance of Jyp as he staggered through the door, panting. Wiping his forehead, he fought to get his breath back. 'Can't explain now. If anyone asks for me tell them I'm out...I've emigrated...tell 'em anything you like.'

Looking bewildered, Julie asked, 'What's happened to Mr Grimshaw - is he with you?'

'Never mind Grimshaw,' Jyp gasped. 'You don't understand, I've got to hide - she's after me!'

'Who is?' Julie persisted, trying to get some sense out of him.

'It's that she-devil, Patience - she's appeared out of the blue. I can't get away from her. You've got to help me, Julie.'

'Well, don't stand there - Grimshaw will be back in a minute.' Julie tried to be practical in an attempt to calm him down. 'Why don't you find somewhere upstairs - I know, what about that office he was going to give you. You can see the street from there. Go on,' as he hesitated, 'you can tell me about it later. Hurry up, I think that's Grimshaw.'

Jyp hesitated no longer. 'Thanks.' He shot her a look of gratitude and vanished from sight, just as Grimshaw arrived out of breath.

'Have you seen Jefferson?' he demanded. 'The man must be mad. One minute he was there and the next he disappeared. Has he returned?'

'If you give me a moment, I will make some enquiries, sir,' she replied diplomatically. 'Meanwhile, can I get you a cup of tea? I'll bring you one right away.'

'Yes, do that,' he wriggled his foot experimentally. 'I think I've sprained my ankle, chasing after that young idiot. I think I'll go and sit down.' As he turned away limping, he ordered, 'Tell him I want to see him immediately he returns.'

'Yes, sir,' she soothed. 'Directly I see him – and I'll bring you a bandage for your ankle.'

Mollified, Grimshaw made his way slowly in the direction of his office.

Upstairs, Jyp peered fearfully out of the window, then unable to see anything leaned out over the sill to get a better view.

Almost immediately a shout of recognition went up. 'Jyp! It's me – Patience! Yoo-hoo!'

Trembling, Jyp ducked down out of sight, knocking over a chair in his panic.

In his office below, Grimshaw was just raising a cup of tea to his lips when the sudden clatter in the room above made him spill the contents over his suit.

'Julie,' he cried as she poked her head in, 'what the devil is that noise?'

'It's probably the mice after we cleaned that office out,' she offered hopefully.

'Nonsense. There's someone up there – I can hear him.' He winced as he tried to get up and cried out petulantly, 'Well, someone go and see.'

'Yes, sir, right away. I'll ask Reg, who serves in the shop.'

Curbing her curiosity, Julie decided that it was not a matter that could be explained very easily over the phone and instead made her way down to the shop, rehearsing in her mind what to say.

'He did – what?' Reg's face emerged astonished from a sea of half opened packets strewn around him on the floor.

'I know it sounds a little odd,' Julie apologised, 'but Mr Grimshaw was quite insistent.

I think it would be better coming from you, Reg,' she added persuasively. 'Jyp seems to have a thing about women at the moment.' Then giving up, she admitted, 'I don't know what's come over him.'

'Ok, Miss Julie. Half a mo' while I climb out of this rubbish.' Clambering up, he gave her a sympathetic grin. 'Don't worry, I'll go and sort it out – I expect this place is getting him down. It happens to all of us in the end.'

Crouching down below the window, Jyp was just experimenting with a small mirror tied to a stick he'd discovered in one of the desk drawers and was poking it up to get a better view of the street when a tap at the door made him drop it. Picking up the pieces with a muttered curse, Jyp was still sucking his hand when a cautious head poked around the door.

'It's me, Reg. Ok to come in?'

'Yes, but keep your head down. I don't want anyone to see me.'

Reg looked around the empty room, bewildered. 'Who's going to - in here?'

'Not here, you idiot. In the street. See if you can see a woman down there.'

Peering out, Reg shook his head. 'A couple of dozen, as far as I can see. What does she look like?'

Heaving a sigh, Jyp scrambled up and using Reg as a shield had a quick peep over his shoulder and shuddered.

'She's still there. What am I going to do?'

Reg shook his head doubtfully. 'Far be it for me to tell you, chum, but from what I gather the old man is doing his nut down there and if you don't go and find out what he wants, Miss Julie will be in trouble.'

That did it. Jyp took a deep breath and straightened his shoulders. 'In that case I'd better go and explain.'

Reg patted him on the back. 'Off you go. Here you are, have a swig of this to keep you going.' He handed over a flask. 'Blimey, you need it to keep sane in this place.'

Swallowing a mouthful, Jyp coughed and handed it back gratefully. 'Thanks, Reg.'

'That's the stuff. Let me know if you want any help and I'll think up an excuse to lend a hand. I'll even bring me smartphone and count the bodies.'

'I might need that.' Jyp pulled a face and made for the door.

'Ah, there you are Jefferson, at last.' Grimshaw sat up with a grimace at the sound of his knock. 'I've got a bone to pick with you. What the devil happened out there? It was supposed to be for your benefit – all it's done is to give me a ricked ankle. Explain yourself.'

Before answering, Jyp edged closer to the window and took a quick glance, hoping against hope she might have given up and gone home. At that moment, the traffic moved on again, revealing Patience still there. Before he could move away, she scanned the windows again and catching sight of him, began to wave frantically. Against his will, he watched fascinated as she unzipped a bag and produced a megaphone she'd borrowed off the tour guide.

'It's me – Patience! Can you hear me? I know you're there!'

Jyp shuddered and bent down, praying she'd give up and go away.

Unfortunately, it had the opposite effect. The announcement was so loud, it echoed up and down the street, causing passersby to stop and look up to see where she was pointing. And even more embarrassing was the alarmed reaction from his boss.

'What is going on down there? Who is that woman?'

Taking another quick glance, Jyp panicked. 'She's after me!'

As everyone knows, the head of one of the country's top security department – and a frontline one at that – is not in the habit of showing fear in the face of adversity but nobody had taken the trouble to tell Mr Grimshaw. Infected by Jyp's actions, he found himself drawn to the window, forgetting about his ankle in his quest for information.

Moistening his lips, he asked nervously, 'What does she want?'

Jyp swallowed. 'She wants me to...'

'To what?'

'To marry her.'

Grimshaw straightened up and dusted himself down with a sigh of relief. 'Why didn't you say so - is that all? My dear man, there's no need hide away like this. Go and talk to her in a sensible manner and reason with her. She can't bite you.'

Jyp gave a hollow groan. 'I've tried that. I've even told her I'm gay to put her off.'

'What did she say to that?'

'She chased me down the corridor and threatened to kill me!'

The other coughed. 'Well, that is a little unusual, I must admit. Come now, let me go down with you and have a few words with this young lady.' He waved a hand tolerantly. 'We can't have this sort of disturbance going on outside our own office. Come now – I must insist.'

Terrified at the prospect, Jyp raised a stricken face, desperate to think of an excuse.

Feeling the effects of the drink, he glanced out again and for a moment, he thought he saw double. Two images of Patience wavered up and down in front of his befuddled gaze as he clung to the window, before blending into one again. In a flash of inspiration, he blurted out. 'It's not just her – it's her cousin, she's even worse. She's vowed to get her own back because she suffered at the hands of some man. She wants to kill me as well.'

Grimshaw gave an amused laugh. 'And who is this other lady who terrifies you? Does she have a name?'

Jyp swallowed. 'She's called Maggie.'

At mention of the name, the superior smile he was wearing was instantly wiped away and the next moment he was crouching next to Jyp, plucking at his sleeve.

'M-Maggie, did you say? Are you sure?'

Grasping at the lifeline, Jyp cast his mind back to the details his Aunt had discovered.

'Yes,' he recalled with relish. 'Apparently some man – a PT instructor, I'm told, led her astray and her mother has never forgiven him.' Looking up innocently, he exclaimed, 'Why, that's what you used to be, weren't you, Mr Grimshaw?'

'Never mind that, Jefferson – that's nothing to do with it,' his boss said hastily.

They were interrupted by a sudden shout outside. Trembling, Grimshaw urged. 'Go and see what they want, Jefferson. Hurry, man.'

Obediently, Jyp raised himself and peered out cautiously. 'There's quite a crowd out there now. Oh, wait a minute, she's holding up some sort of a message.'

'What does it say, man?'

'Just trying to see...something about wanting justice. I think she's trying to get them to storm the building.'

'We've got the stop them – what can we do?' Grimshaw looked around desperately, seeking a solution. 'I know,' he hobbled over to his desk and grabbed a bundle of bank notes. 'Here, Jefferson, see if this will stop them.'

He piled them up in Jyp's arms and pointed at the window. 'Hurry up man, I can't do it – see if this lot will get rid of them. This damned ankle of mine is killing me.' His face paled at his unfortunate choice of words.

Blinking, Jyp prised the window open and threw out the money, creating a shower of notes as they fluttered down at a row of astonished faces below.

'Well, what are they saying?'

Making the most of the opportunity Jyp cocked an ear at the window and turned back, raising his hands. 'It's no good, they're after blood.' He paused to see how it went down, and remembering something Reg had told him when they first met, he crossed his fingers.

'I believe she said her mother used to be on the stage with some sort of knife act – that's before she had to give it up because of her eyesight, of course.'

Grimshaw gulped and clutched his arm. 'Is she down there now?'

Taking another look, Jyp reported brightly. 'I think so, there's someone practicing on a sandbag. Said something about wanting a confession and getting the police.'

'The police!' Grimshaw fell on his knees. 'You've got to stop them. You don't understand.' His words started pouring out in his frantic efforts to get it off his chest. 'I'll do anything to keep that woman away. I never wanted to get into this spying business in the first place. It was all because of that woman.'

Just then, the door opened and Reg poked his head in. 'Excuse me sir, there's a police sergeant outside would like a word.'

Jyp clicked his fingers to attract his attention, and held his hands up, going through the motions of taking a picture. Hoping that Reg would get the message, he turned soothingly to Grimshaw. 'I'm sure they'll understand, sir. Now, what were you saying - something about being blackmailed? Who was that?'

Grimshaw grasped the straw and started gabbling, 'It was all C's fault. I never wanted to be part of it. He made me smuggle all those illegals in, otherwise he threatened to expose me.'

His voice trailed off as he caught sight of Reg's smartphone and he stopped, appalled at how easily he had been tricked. Summoning up his scattered wits, he forgot all about his ankle in a frantic effort to get away, pausing only scoop up a bundle of notes as he dived for the door, slamming it shut behind him.

Handing over his smartphone, Reg summed up the situation with a grin. 'That's what I call an open and shut case!'

Chapter Eight

A Night to Remember

Rushing in to see what was going on, Julie caught sight of Jyp trying to pull himself up, and flew to his side.

'Oh, Jyp, sweetheart, are you all right – did he hurt you?'

'No, I'm ok, honest,' Jyp protested, pulling himself together. 'Did you say sweetheart?'

'Never mind that,' she scolded, sniffing the air and stepping back. 'You've been drinking!'

Reg hurried forward, giving his support. 'Only a tiny drop, Miss Julie, just to help him recover from the boss – our ex-boss, I should say,' he corrected himself.

Julie looked around, bewildered. 'What's been going on? Where's Mr Grimshaw? It looks as if a cyclone has hit the place.'

'He's scarpered, that's what,' crowed Reg with satisfaction, holding up his smartphone. 'Thanks to Jyp we've got all the evidence we need. Listen to this.'

He played back details of the confession made by Grimshaw.

'Is this true?' Julie turned to Jyp, her face lighting up. 'How did you manage that?'

'Well, I just reminded him about some of his shady goings-on,' Jyp began modestly.

But before he could continue, Julie threw her arms around his neck gleefully. 'This means no more of his wretched dictation. I knew there was something fishy about him. Look at all that money he was flashing around, which reminds me, that sergeant is still waiting outside for an explanation of all that money that came out the window - it caused an almighty traffic jam outside. I'd better go and see him.'

As she was leaving, she looked over her shoulder. 'By the way, that friend of yours left a note for you on my desk. You'd better come and see what she says.'

Swallowing, Jyp followed her nervously and with trembling hands opened the envelope.

Meanwhile, Julie managed to placate the sergeant with a hurried explanation and a promise to make a full report, then shut the door behind him and leaned against it with a sigh of relief.

'Well, that's that. Now,' she turned to Jyp eager to hear his news, 'what does she say – has she given up chasing you, or are we expecting another visit?'

She prodded him as he sat there with glazed look on his face, lost to the world.

'Come on, tell us the worst.'

'Eh?' Jyp came to slowly, and spoke feebly, 'you'll never guess.'

'Hurry up, I've got to ring Head Office to tell them the dreaded news.'

'After all that chasing, all she wanted to tell me was...'

'Go on, spill the beans. No, don't tell me,' she guessed, 'she's threatening to go into a convent.'

'No, she's decided to get married!' he managed, with a blissful look on his face.

'What? How can she, while you're holed up in here?'

'I don't mean me,' he hastily corrected her. 'She's had a proposal from Mr. Benson, of all people!'

'What? I thought he was her boss – he must be old enough to be her father, from what you were saying.'

'I don't care how old he is – she's marrying old Benson!' he waved his arms gleefully. 'That means I'm free. Who would have believed it!'

'Well, now we've sorted out that little problem, what are you going to send her for a wedding present?'

He looked up sheepishly. 'She says thanks to all that money we chucked out of the window it's going to pay for the whole bang shoot – wedding reception and the lot.'

'Well, I don't think we'd better mention that in our report,' decided Julie thoughtfully.

'I think we'd better break the news about Grimshaw and call it a day. I can't wait to tell Dad about it. Golly, this'll give them something to talk about up in Head Office. I wonder who they'll think up next?'

* * *

By a strange coincidence that particular subject was under discussion later that day at the very heart of the establishment.

'I say, Binky, what's all this about old Grimshaw, your brother-in-law? They tell me on the grapevine he's come a nasty cropper.'

'Don't remind me, old chap. It's all doom and gloom at yours truly.'

'Doom and gloom? Why, what's happened?'

'Just because we gave him the job – you'd think the Missus would be grateful.'

'And wasn't she?'

'She was until old Grimshaw did a bunk.'

'Why was that?'

'They found out he was letting in the illegals, instead of keeping them out.'

'So that didn't go down well.'

'She said it was all our fault giving him the job in the first place – I even had to go without my comforts.'

'You poor old thing.'

'I mean my toast and marmalade – she only gave me one slice this morning. Just shows you.'

'Never mind – at least we won't see him doing his rotten old Father Christmas act at our place any more.'

'And all because of that new man down there, I hear.'

'Yes, I'm happy to say that was one of our best moves, bringing him in.'

'Don't be modest, Binky, it was a brilliant move of yours.'

'Oh, I wouldn't say that, Trevor, old man.'

'But Binky, you know very well nobody will go near the place since he's been there. Old Blenkinsock in Personnel tells me he's had half a dozen or so spies clamouring to give themselves up as soon as they heard we had their names down for the job.'

'True. He's done some first class work there. What was his name, Jyp, or something?'

'Yes, if you remember he did his time at Watlington Grammar.'

'Well, I suppose we can't hold that against him.'

'Do you know, Binky, if you don't mind me saying, I think we ought to make the most of his success in the short time he's been down there - even if he did go to that ghastly school they all talk about. I know, why don't we invite him up for the next Embassy affair – it would do the old Department no end of a boost. Get us some good Brownie points, I shouldn't wonder – goodness knows, we could do with some.'

'Now, why didn't I think of that?'

'You can't think of everything at the same time, Binky old chap. Let's face it, you're head and shoulders above the rest of us. I sometimes think you ought to give that old brainbox of yours a bit of a rest – you don't want to get fagged out before Goodwood comes up.'

'I know, old man, you're quite right. I often wonder what they'd do without me. And while we're at it, what about that nice young secretary down there - perhaps we could persuade her to come as well. We could do with a bit of talent at these social do's. You must admit, they can be a bit of a bore - remember what happened when old Brigadier Whats-his-name turned up.'

'Especially if they all get sloshed, like they did last time. I'd better book some rooms so that they can stay over and sleep it off.'

'Good thinking, Trevor, old chap.'

'Don't give it another thought. Leave it to me, Binky old man. I'll fix it all up.'

'I knew I could rely on you, Trevor. See you at the club later?'

'I should hope so, Binkey. My turn tonight.'

* * *

The day of the Embassy Ball arrived with a fanfare of trumpets. It was considered to be the social affair of the season. Strings were pulled and discreet telephone calls were made until everyone who considered they had a right to be there were invited.

Unaccustomed to such events, Julie was all of a twitter getting ready for the evening and kept on imploring Jyp to tell her if she was all right every few minutes until it was time to leave.

Reassured on that point and after giving Jyp a critical inspection, Julie entrusted him with a holdall carrying her expensive high-heeled shoes she was intending to change into as soon as they arrived, and crossed her fingers hoping Jyp would not be led astray by any more females.

Directly they arrived their presence was announced by a flunkey at the door and our two security officials who had been waiting breathlessly rushed up to welcome them.

'Here you are then,' crowed the first one, beating the other by a short head. 'My turn, Binky. Don't tell me, you must be Jefferson…Pratbottom – the man they're all talking about?'

'Patbottom,' corrected Jyp automatically.

'You poor thing, never mind,' sympathised Trevor archly, patting Jyp's arm. 'Let me introduce you to my boss – just call him Sir Archibald, if you don't mind. He'd prefer not to be called by his full title – security, you understand.' Then coyly, 'You can call me Trevor.'

'Sir Archibald?' smiled Jyp nervously, 'how do you do? Turning to Julie. 'May I present Miss Diamond, our chief secretary?'

'It's a great pleasure,' interrupted Sir Archibald hastily. 'We've heard all about the splendid work you're doing, isn't that right, Trevor?'

'Indeed, Binky. And we've got all sorts of people who are dying to meet you.'

'Good, then I'll leave you to do the honours, Trevor old man,' said Binky catching sight of someone waving at him. 'If you'll excuse me, I'll catch up with you in a moment.'

'Follow me, let's see who we have...Oh, my word, it's the Brigadier, this way.' He steered them hastily in a new direction, accidentally bumping into a bored looking guest smoking a cigar.

'Ah, just the fellow, Charles. This is an extraordinary coincidence. Let me introduce you to our latest recruit, Jefferson Pratbottom, who is getting splendid results down at our latest screening centre on the coast.'

The two men eyed each other warily. 'How do you do,' offered Jyp, holding out a hand.

Flapping his hand languidly, the other replied, 'Glad to meet you,' then catching sight of Julie, his interest quickened. 'And who is this charming young lady?'

Pleased to have gained an audience, Trevor prattled on, 'This is Miss Diamond who is in charge of the all secretarial services down there, I understand.'

'How do you do, Miss Diamond – how very nice to meet you,' greeted the newcomer, bending over and kissing her hand, much to her embarrassment.

'Well now,' Trevor enthused, ignoring their guest's searching gaze, 'this is a fortunate coincidence. It's not often we have the chance of bringing together one of our leading spy heads,' nodding to Charles, 'and one of our latest spy catchers,' waving at Jyp.

There was a brief pause in the conversation as they weighed each other up. Then Charles waved a self-deprecating hand. 'Not just at the moment, Trevor. I've completed my normal tour and I'm on the look-out for fresh fields to investigate. What about you, Pratbottom?'

'Patbottom,' Jyp corrected hastily. 'I'm only a newcomer at the game, I'm afraid. Still learning the ropes. I'm counting on this new job to add up to something worthwhile.'

'Ah, then you still have a lot to take in, I see.'

Before either could think of anything else to say, they were interrupted by a breezy figure joining them.

'You young fellers don't know what spying's all about. Now, when I was in India – that was the place to be. Did I ever tell you?'

Noticing the bored expression on Julie's face, Charles offered an arm, 'Would you care for some refreshments, Miss Diamond, and perhaps a turn around the floor?'

Glad at the opportunity of getting away from what promised to be a tedious discussion of old times, Julie quickly agreed, after a reproachful look at Jyp.

Delighted to have an audience at last, the Brigadier smoothed his whiskers at the prospect. Ignoring their trapped expressions he got down to it in earnest. After five minutes Trevor thought up an excuse and broke away hurriedly, leaving Jyp at his mercy.

'Ah, what say about a hair of the dog, eh Pratbottom – waiter? I say, young feller did I ever tell you about the time we were holed up in the Kyber Pass with only a couple of bearers between us and the damned rebels breathing down our necks?'

Hastily closing his hand over his glass after what seemed hours later to prevent any more refills from the ever attentive waiters, Jyp found himself swaying backwards and forwards, mesmerised by the actions of the Brigadier who was waving his hands like a conjuror to illustrate the tactics his force used when they were fighting back to back and surrounded by the enemy.

Just as he was wondering how much more he could stand, a slim hand slid under his arm and a seductive voice crooned, 'Now, Brigadier, don't commandeer our guests, you naughty man, or he'll have nobody else to talk to. Now who is this gorgeous man– I don't think I have the pleasure, Mr...?'

'Patbottom - Jefferson,' Jyp answered, glad of the interruption.

'Ah, you're the one they're all talking about.' She squeezed his arm. 'Come with me, Jefferson, or can I call you, Jeff?'

'Of course,' he gulped, casting a quick look around to see if Julie could see them.

'I'm Simone, by the way,' she fluttered her eyes at him, 'in case you wondered. Let's get away from all these stuffy old men and get ourselves a drink somewhere nice and cosy, all by ourselves and you can tell me all about yourself. Waiter, the usual, please!'

Later, when at last he managed to collect his scattered wits together, he found himself in an even worse position, wedged as he was against the bar stool with her barely concealed bosom pressed against him. Wondering how he had managed to get in such a compromising situation Jyp glanced around wildly, trying to think up a convincing excuse to get away. After a few of the barman's specials, however, his resistance began to weaken and who knows what might have happened if his companion had not at that moment receive an urgent summons. With a muttered apology, Simone slid down from her seat and joined someone standing almost out of sight at the bar entrance. Raising his bleary eyes, Jyp attempted to make out the features of her companion. As he turned away after a brief exchange between the two, Jyp saw it was Charles, the mystery spy chief.

Hastily re-joining him, Simone was profuse in apologies. 'I have to go now, Jyp, but I will be back later. Meanwhile, this is my room number – you know where to find me. Give me a call.' She searched his eyes with a devouring glance. 'Promise.'

Jyp mumbled. 'If I can,' promising to himself that it was the last thing he would dream of doing.

What seemed like hours later, Jyp managed to raise his head from the counter to find the lights dimmed and the barman waiting to close the bar. Staggering to his feet with an effort, he made his way to the reception and asked for the key to his room.

Handing it over, the reception girl apologised that the bathroom in his room was out of order, and handed him a key to another bathroom along the corridor. Pocketing it, he thanked her owlishly and staggered off, leaving the clerk shaking her head.

As he climbed into bed and closed his eyes with a blissful sigh of relief, all he could think about was what had happened to Julie and that bounder Charles who couldn't keep his eyes off her all evening.

Later he woke after dreaming he was being chased by Simone and she was getting closer and closer.'

Finding an urgent need to visit the bathroom, he rolled out of bed and padded along the corridor looking for the right door. Misreading the number on the key he tried one of the doors without success and was just turning away when the door opened and he came face to face with the Brigadier.

'Ah, in need of another sniffer, eh? Come in, my dear chap and join me for a quick one – I was looking for an excuse to open another bottle.'

'No, no,' said Jyp panic stricken, 'I was looking for the bathroom.'

'Ah, well on second thoughts it might be better if you use the one down the corridor. I'd offer you our facilities but the memsahib has only just got her head down and we might disturb her.'

Wiping his face, Jyp tottered back down the corridor and thinking he recognised the door tried the key again. This time the door opened before he could get the key out and a familiar face appeared. It was Simone.

Before he could offer an apology and escape, a hand came out and janked him in.

'Why, Jeff, how lovely. And there was I thinking you'd forgotten all about me.'

'No, no, I didn't mean to…it's all a mistake. I thought it was my room.'

'Never mind, you're here – that's all that matters. Come and sit down here on the couch and make yourself comfortable while I get the drinks.'

'But I can assure you,' he began, panicked, and backing to the door.

'Oh, you meannie, you're not going to desert me? I've been waiting for you so long.

Here, just a teenie one then for old time's sake, I'm sure you can manage that.' As she poured a generous helping she slipped a tablet in the glass and shook it before handing it over.

Jyp cautiously took a sip and getting an encouraging smile managed another before slumping back on his seat and letting the glass slide out of his hand. Simone quickly scooped it up with a smile of triumph and peeling back the bedclothes started to undress him.

Waking up in the night, he shook his head groggily and gazed around trying to remember where he was. Feeling around cautiously his hand came into contact with warm flesh and he jumped up petrified.

Then the light came on and he realised his worst nightmare had come true. It was Simone and she was wearing nothing except a smile of happy expectation.

'Oh, darling, I've been waiting so long for this moment. I can see you have too.'

'No! I mean, what am I doing here? It's all a mistake.'

'Oh, you're not going so soon when we were just getting to know each other, darling.' Her hand slid across and she nestled up against him.

Holding back a scream, Jyp leapt out of the bed and searched around frantically for his pyjamas, trying to put them on as he dived for the door.

'But dearest. Don't leave me!'

'I must go,' he babbled. 'I, er, promised to phone...'

'What, at this time of night?'

'I can't stay here, the maid will find out.'

'Well, give me your room number and I'll come and see you instead.'

Anxious to leave, he blurted out the first number that came into his head and headed for the door.

Outside, he barged into the reception girl again who gave him a frigid look.

'Can I help you, sir?'

'I've...er...forgotten my room number.'

She consulted her list and sniffed suspiciously, as if she'd heard that tale a thousand times before. 'Really – your name?'

'Er, Patbottom.'

'Here we are, just opposite, Room 134. Will that be all?' She eyed him sternly, making him feel like a naughty schoolboy up before the Head.

'Yes,' he mumbled, searching for some change. 'Sorry, I don't seem to have any...'

'Quaite,' she tossed her head disdainfully, making a mental note to report him to the management. 'Good night, sir.'

* * *

A somewhat groggy imitation of Jyp made his way down in the lift to the breakfast room the next morning. Peering around the door he was relieved to see Julie sitting alone at a table and hurried over to join her.

'Hello, Jyp. What on earth happened to you last night. You completely disappeared – I was quite worried.'

He sat down gingerly and relaxed after a hasty glance around for signs of Simone. 'It was all a bit hazy,' he confessed. 'I think I must have overdone it a bit on the drinks.'

Julie sniffed and gave him a hopeless look. 'Oh, Jyp, what are we going to do with you. You reek of it.'

'I'll feel better after a coffee,' he admitted hopefully. Changing the subject, he counter-attacked. 'And what about you? I saw that Charles character giving you the glad eye.'

'Oh, Jyp,' she looked dreamy, 'he's such a wonderful dancer, you've no idea.' She eyed him frankly. 'You never asked me for a dance – not once.'

'I didn't get a chance,' grumbled Jyp. 'I'll make up for it,' he promised. 'I seem to have got distracted by other things,' and he gave a hasty glance around to make sure they were alone.

As they collected their holdall at the desk he took a last look around, and thought to himself at least they wouldn't be bothered by that man again, thank goodness. Just as he was about to add, "or anyone else", the lady he had been dreading appeared at the entrance, arguing with two attendants carrying her luggage and trying in vain to flag down a taxi at the same time.

'Oh look, Jyp, there's that lady you were dancing with – why don't we offer her a lift?'

Swallowing, Jyp took refuge behind a newspaper and prayed she hadn't seen them.

To his overwhelming relief, a taxi appeared around the corner and Simone flagged it down imperiously and gave directions to the perspiring porters before jumping in.

'Did you see that? She must have known we were here first. Of all the cheek!'

Grateful for the change of heart, Jyp hurriedly stepped out in front of the next taxi that had to pile on its brakes to avoid hitting him.

'Well done, darling. Thank goodness we've seen the last of her,' was Julie's verdict.

Jyp wholeheartedly agreed with her, but all the same had an uneasy suspicion they hadn't heard the last of her.

Chapter Nine

Best Man

Although they thought they had seen the last of Simone, she undoubtedly left an indelible impression in the upper reaches of Whitehall, as our two top officials were ready to testify.

'I sat Trevor old man, what was all that kerfuffle about at the do last night?'

'Oh you didn't hear – I thought the whole of the hotel knew about it.'

'Well, what with one thing and another, it was all a bit heavy going – so many people to see and things to do.'

'I know, Binky, I don't know how you manage – what with all your responsibilities.'

'Never mind that, fill me in, Trevor – fill me in.'

'Right, you know that Simone from that embassy of hers, wherever it is.'

'You mean that slinky looking one. I mean that attractive lady with the big...um portfolio?'

'Well, two portfolios to be strictly accurate, old man. Anyway, I heard this from the young lady at the reception desk – awfully upset, she was.'

'Yes, I'm sure she would be...but what happened?'

'I'm telling you. Apparently, in the middle of the night Simone went and knocked on the door of ...wait for it...our friend the Brigadier.'

'No.'

'It's a fact. Flimsy nightie and all, and this is the best bit.'

'Can't wait, go on.'

'Well, instead of the Brigadier, she got his missus!'

'No, what did Simone have to say?'

'Oh, some cock and bull story about looking for someone else.'

'I bet that didn't go down very well.'

'I should cocoa – the Missus was livid. Said she always suspected he was seeing some tart or other.'

'And had he?'

'The Brigadier? You're joking, the last time he got involved with any sporting activity was in the Indian Mutiny days when he was potting off tigers from the back of an elephant.'

'So how did it finish up?'

'Well, it all ended up in a slanging match. They were making so much noise, half the corridor could hear – even the old Brigadier tottered out to see what was up. The net result was old Simone got recalled by her Embassy and I doubt whether the Brigadier will dare show his face again at any more of our do's.'

'That's something to be grateful for, I suppose. A pity about that Simone though – she knew how to get things off with a swing, um, I meant get things going, hem, socially, of course.'

'I know what you mean, Binky – don't we all. That friend of yours, that super spy chap, was livid about it – he was a great friend of hers apparently.'

'Was he now? That reminds me, he seemed very interested in that problem of ours down at Plumpton.'

'I know, he couldn't keep his eyes off her, I noticed.'

'No, I was talking about getting a replacement for old Grimshaw – he was particularly keen on taking on the challenge.'

'Yes, smashing piece of work, wasn't she.'

'Anyway, I jumped at the chance – not often we see one of our best spies teaming up with one of our best spy catchers, is it?'

'I say, I have to hand it to you, Binky old man – you've done it again.'

'Nice of you to say so, Trevor, I wonder how they'll get on together.'

'If it's one of your ideas, Binky, it can't possibly fail.'

* * *

There was a message waiting for Jyp and Julie back at the office saying that their new boss would be joining them the next day.

'I wonder who it will be this time?' sighed Julie. 'I suppose it will be another of those retirement types they take off the shelves and give a dusting down.'

'I must tell my aunt all about it – she must have come across quite a few when she was in the service,' agreed Jyp.

'Well, there's no point hanging around here,' decided Julie. 'I'll just check the office and make sure it looks tidy and then we might as well go home.'

After a quick inspection, Jyp was about to close the door behind him when a piece of paper caught by the draft fluttered down to the floor. Picking it up Jyp stuffed it in his pocket, meaning to look at it later, and promptly forgot about it before joining her at the exit.

* * *

It was not until next morning when his aunt came across it after putting his trousers in the wash that he remembered.

'What's this?' his aunt wanted to know. 'Looks like some sort of a message – what's left of it, after it's been in the washing machine. Sorry about that. Here, have a look.'

Jyp picked up the tattered remnants and whistled. 'Crickey, someone had it in for old Grimshaw. He's telling him to cough up, or get it in the neck. Signed,' he peered at the faded handwriting, 'looks like a capital 'C'.

'C', eh?'repeated his Aunt thoughtfully. 'That sounds like one of the shorthand signals they used to use in Bomber Command – 'C' for Charlie, and all that sort of thing.'

'Before my time,' said Jyp cheekily.

'That's as may be,' commented his aunt. 'But that's all we've got to go on at the moment.

We'll just have to wait and find out who this new boss of yours is and see if he can throw any light on it.'

Directly he got into the office it was buzzing with speculation about who he would be.

Julie was optimistic after hearing rumours over the phone and was hugging herself in anticipation, bursting to pass on the gossip.

'Spill the beans, Miss,' urged Reg, as he caught a hint of her excitement.

'All I hear is that he's much younger than our previous Head,' Julie cautioned, then unable to keep it to herself she giggled, 'but they say he's awfully handsome,' giving Jyp a sideways glance to see how he reacted.

But Jyp was already pouring over a letter he had just received and was growing paler by the minute at the contents.

'What's up, Jyp?' she asked sweetly, hoping to share some good news.

'It's nothing,' he swallowed, stuffing it away quickly. 'Nothing important.'

He stood there unable to think for a moment, then, 'I'm sorry, something's come up. I must pop out for a moment.' Seeing her questioning look, he added hurriedly, 'My aunt.'

'Nothing wrong, is there?'

'No, no.' he wiped his brow. 'I'll tell you about it later.'

'Well, give her our love,' but the rest of her words were lost as he shot out of the office and staggered down the stairs. Outside, he leant for a moment against the front door wondering what on earth he should do. Snatching another glance at the letter he read the last sentence again, 'Have broken it off with Howard. Must see you at once. Meet you outside at ten o'clock.' He checked the letter again to make sure he wasn't dreaming and shuddered at the sight of the signature - 'Patience'. The thought of Julie finding out and going through all that again...Urrg. And coming on top of that ghastly episode at the hotel with Simone. The mind boggled.

A few minutes later after pacing up and down he caught sight of her familiar figure bearing down on him. Casting a hasty glance around and seeing the entrance to the cafe he'd been in only recently with Julie he summoned up a weak smile of welcome and grabbing her arm pulled her in.

Over a quick cup of coffee to steady his nerves, he endured a long and garbled account of how Mr Benson, or Howard as she called him, had been treating her and how he kept on changing his mind and how he had left her to organise everything and what a terrible mess everything was in and how she had missed her precious moments with her old friend, Jefferson, pressing his arm to emphasise her words, 'her dearest friend and the only one who had stood by her and understood how she really felt.'

Unable to stand any more, Jyp cut her short. 'What happened?'

Seeing her long winded explanations were wasted Patient reluctantly came to the point.

'His best man has been posted overseas and he can't find anyone to replace him. What can we do? You will help us, won't you, Jefferson? There's no one else I can ask.'

Jyp gulped. 'You don't mean...'

'Oh, I knew I could count on you, dear Jefferson. Otherwise, there will be just the two of us left on the shelf together again, just like old times. Wouldn't that be fun. But I mustn't raise your hopes, dear man. You must be brave and sacrifice your longings and know your selfless action will ensure my future happiness.' She pressed a file into his quivering hands. 'There, I knew you wouldn't let me down. All the details are there. Two o' clock tomorrow afternoon at Finsbury Circus, you can't miss it. And now I must fly, byee.'

Jyp slowly made his way back to the office, his mind in a ferment. What if he agreed to step in as best man. Supposing Howard changed his mind at the last moment, he would be expected to do the decent thing and fill the gap - anything but that. But if he didn't - his tortured brain tottered at the appalling prospect - Patience would be free to pursue him all over again. It was no good, he would have to bite the bullet and tell Julie. But first, he needed a stiff drink to help him face up to the task.

But to no avail. When he attempted to tell her when he got back to the office, she brushed aside his explanations in her eagerness about their new boss.

'Who would have imagined it,' she greeted him excitedly. 'It turns out that it's that super spy we met at the embassy do – that dishy man, Charles Morris.'

'Oh, a Morris dancer, eh Miss?' quipped Reg, overhearing.

'No, he's a wonderful dancer,' said Julie coldly. 'There goes his bell again – I must see what he wants.' With that, she checked her make-up in the mirror and scooping up her shorthand notebook rushed off to answer the call.

Left to his own devices Jyp brooded on his misfortune. Just as he thought he'd found the girl he had been looking for some smooth character comes along and sweeps her off her feet. As if he didn't have enough to worry about, what with the threat of Patience hanging over him and the memory of that ghastly encounter with Simone at the hotel, it didn't bear thinking about.

His mixed feelings were interrupted by the sight of Julie emerging from Morris's office, her face wreathed in smiles.

'Charles, I mean Mr Morris, wants to see you, Jyp.'

'Oh, all right.' Trying to ignore the fact that she was already on familiar terms with their new boss, Jyp fought back his instinctive dislike of the situation and obeyed the summons.

'Ah, Jefferson.' Morris waved him absently to a chair in front of his desk.

Jyp eyed him warily. He could understand now why Julie found him so fascinating. His sensitive features and wistful brown eyes would have won him an instant audition for any romantic musical in the West End and would have had a bevy of adoring female queuing up and sighing over his autograph.

'You asked to see me, sir.'

'Yes.' His new boss seemed preoccupied. 'I'm sorry, I was just wondering why I hadn't heard from a friend of mine after yesterday. I think you met her at the Embassy do – Simone.'

He waited for a reaction and Jyp felt his eyes boring into him.

Jyp gulped at the memory. 'Yes, I seem to remember, we did kind of bump into each other at some point.'

'Never mind.' Morris let go of the subject reluctantly and studied the paper in front of him. 'We must decide what to do about you.' He laced his fingers together and flexed his hands as if making up his mind. 'I see you went through the "school run" under Major Fanshaw that produced some unusual results.'

Giving a nervous smile of acknowledgement Jyp waited for him to continue, fearing the worst.

'What we need to do now is to get you down to doing something more useful – something that will give you some first hand experience of spy work.' And something, he thought to himself, that would keep this meddlesome brat out of the way so I can have Julie to myself.

'Let me see,' he thought aloud, eyeing Jyp with disfavour, 'there must be something we can find for you to do.' He was about to continue when his musings were interrupted by a loud thumping noise at the window. Looking up, he caught sight of a window cleaner at work, attacking his task with gusto. The grubby state of the shirt he was wearing gave Morris an idea and he strolled over and rapped at the window, nearly causing the man to fall off his ladder.

'You there.' He threw up the casement.

A face appeared cautiously after the man regained his hold with difficulty. 'What, me, guv?'

'Yes, come in here a moment.'

'Nothing wrong, is there, guv? If it's about that broken pane last time it was just an accident – not my fault, the ladder slipped, honest, guv.'

'Nothing like that. Just hand over your shirt and trousers.'

'You're joking, guv. How am I going to manage without them - it's draughty out here.'

'Nonsense, you've got underwear – pants and vest, haven't you?'

'Give over, guv – I'll get arrested.'

'Here,' Morris thrust a note at him impatiently. 'Will that do?'

The window cleaner held it up and kissed it. 'Why didn't you say so before?' With some difficulty, he wriggled out of his shirt and passed it over. Then he clambered into the room and stepped out of his trousers. 'What's this, some sort of a game, guv?'

'Never you mind – don't say anything about this, mind you.'

The window cleaner shivered and hopped up onto the window ledge and called back. 'You can rely on me, guv. Don't go in for those sort of games myself, mind.'

'There you are.' Morris dumped the rumpled items of clothing on the desk in front of Jyp with a sniff. 'Just the job.'

'What, me?' Jyp picked up the shirt looking slightly bemused. 'What do I do with these?'

Morris snapped impatiently. 'Put them on, of course. Now what I want you to do,' as Jyp hesitated, 'is to sit outside in this lot and pretend you're down on your luck and out of work.'

Jyp's head emerged through the neck of the shirt and he blinked, completely mystified.

'What's the idea?'

'One of the rules of being a good spy is being able to pass yourself off in any situation, whatever you're wearing. Excellent training. Let me see,' he glanced at his watch and coughed. 'I have an important engagement, otherwise I would have been around personally to check on your progress. But keep at it,' he beamed, his temper restored at the thought of his luncheon date. 'I shall want a report directly I get back. Remember,' he patted Jyp on his back, being careful not to soil his hands in the process, 'it's for the good of the service and will make a man of you. Meanwhile,' as he escorted Jyp to the door, 'I will lock up here and make sure your clothes are perfectly safe. Off you go – I'll be thinking of you.'

That may have been his initial intention, but as Jyp took up his position outside in his new buskers outfit and upturned cap at his side, he noticed that Morris had conveniently forgotten about all about him as he escorted Julie off to lunch without a backward glance.

If you've ever had the misfortune to play the part of a down and out in a smelly old outfit that has passed through a number of hands on its journey through life, my advice it to think again, long and hard – there's no future in it.

Evidently the majority of the public who passed by thought so as well, because after one or two had dropped the odd coin in his cap and had hurried on after a quick sniff, life resumed its uneventful nature.

All except for the owner of the shop, who, informed of his presence came out to discover what the disturbance was all about and evidently didn't think much of it. After a furtive glance up and down he leant over and hissed, 'I say, do you mind moving on, you're causing an obstruction, my man.' He would have added a few more pertinent remarks about the tramp's appearance but his customary courtesy forbade it. Taking a closer look he exclaimed, 'Why bless my soul, it's young Jyp – what on earth are you doing here in that peculiar outfit?'

'I was wondering that myself,' replied Jyp gloomily.

'Well, for heaven's sake don't sit there, right in front of my shop – it's bad for trade. Can't you move on – here's something to keep you going.' He thrust a note into Jyp's hand and shaking his head hurried back into the safety of his shop.

Moving on as he was instructed, Jyp was soon pounced on by another irate owner. 'Are you trying to ruin me? Why, it's Jyp from that spy shop – don't they give you enough to live on? After all the rates we pay, it's disgusting. Here, how much do you need?'

Before Jyp realised it he was amassing quite a haul of cash from disgruntled shopkeepers who quickly moved him on, just as he was making himself comfortable. In the end he found had to transfer wads of notes into his pocket to keep abreast of events.

He was just beginning to relax at his unexpected good fortune when the nearby Church clock starting striking and brought him to his senses. Patience! He had forgotten all about her blessed wedding. Oh my God! What was the time? He checked his watch in horror. He was supposed to be at Finsbury Circus at half past two as best man! He fingered his grubby shirt. What the devil was he supposed to do?

Scooping up his cap he hurried back to the office only to find the door to Morris's office was locked. Damn. It was still lunch time so Reg was out and there was nobody else around who could help him. As he stood there his mind racing, he caught sight of the row of models in golfing attire in the shop window and snapped his fingers. Of course!

Without thinking, he stripped off his shirt and trousers and to the startled gaze of a passerby he quickly donned a pair of highly coloured shorts and a striped shirt. Stuffing the notes in his pocket, he offered up a prayer and dashing out, flagged down a taxi.

As he neared the station he consulted his watch for the umpteenth time and wondered whether he was going to make the next fast train to London. When he arrived, he quickly stuffed some notes into the hands of the surprised cabby and bounded up the steps just in time to see the train start to move. Ignoring shouts from the porter, he janked the nearest door open and collapsed inside, making the elderly lady opposite draw her dog towards her protectively.

Getting his breath back, Jyp felt in his shirt for the address and then went through all his other pockets before realising he'd left it in his coat in the office. His groans at the discovery were so heartfelt that the old lady leant over solicitously and offered him a piece of fudge she was about to give to her peke who proceeded to nip her after missing out on the treat.

Cudgelling his mind, Jyp dimly remembered it was somewhere near Finsbury Circus and sank back limply hoping he would have better luck at the other end. Directly the train arrived, Jyp dived out of the carriage and ignoring the queue rapped on the taxi window and cried, 'Doctor – this is an emergency!' Eyeing his clothes dubiously, the cabby decided to give him the benefit of the doubt after seeing his bulging wallet and allowed him in. Pocketing a generous tip, he put his flag up and drove off amid outraged protests from the others waiting patiently.

'Where to, guv?'

Jyp coughed. 'The church near Finsbury Circus – I have... um... a patient needing urgent treatment,' he added feverishly.

'Cor blimey, you do get 'em, don't you, Doc. Keeled over in church did they?' Before he could think of an excuse, the cabby chatted breezily, 'That reminds me of some old geezer I had once who swore he was the King of Ruritania – I had to kneel down before he would cough up.'

'Thanks, this looks like it,' Jyp interrupted him as a church came into view. Drop me off here.' The taxi swerved with a crunch of brakes.

'Blimey, you didn't 'alf give me a turn. Here, do you want me to wait?'

'No, this will do fine,' Jyp assured him, climbing out before the cabby went any further. 'Here, will this do?'

The taxi driver blinked at the size of the tip. 'I should hope so, chum – blimey, I could book a world cruise on this lot.' Watching Jyp scuttle up the steps, he meditated. 'Cripes, in that get-up it's a wonder they don't slip a straight jacket on him and cart him off.' He rubbed his stubbly chin. 'Shall I wait for them to chuck him out? No, my son, quit while you're winning.' Heaving a wistful sigh, he ruminated, 'Mind you, I could do with one or two of him to go on before I retire, fat chance.'

Arriving inside the quiet dignity of the church, Jyp was immediately stopped by a harassed cleaner. 'You're too late.'

'Late?' quavered Jyp. You mean the wedding's over?'

'Wedding? Who said anything about a wedding? This is church cleaning day, and it's finished, dear. You'll find them all down at the pub.'

'But this is three, Church Way, isn't it?' gabbled Jyp, trying to re-member the address he was given.

'No, dear. This is 103, dear. That's up the other end of the road. Someone's given you the wrong one – I ask you, some people can't count. Here,' she peered at Jyp more closely, 'you aren't the one they're all talking about? My cousin told me all about you – Jyp, isn't it? You're quite famous – can I have your autograph?'

But she was talking to thin air. Jyp had fled.

Five minutes down the road Jyp was reassured by the sound of an elderly parishioner peering short-sightedly at the organ, practising his own unorthodox version of the introduction to "The Arrival of the Queen of Sheba".

As he dived thankfully into the porch entrance, muttering, 'Good old Handel, keep it going,' a linesman stepped forward and barred his way. 'Excuse me, sir, tradesmen round the back.'

'Is this the Benson's wedding?' demanded Jyp desperately, grabbing his sleeve.

Pulling his arm away disdainfully, the linesman answered coldly. 'There is a ceremony due to take place for the gentleman you mentioned, but I fail to see how it concerns you.'

'But, but, I'm the best man!' gabbled Jyp. 'Let me in.'

Had he taken time to reflect on the state he was in he might have listened to wiser counsel from his inner self, but conscious of the pressing need to fulfil his obligations Jyp took a chance.

'Look at that!' He directed the man's startled gaze up into the lofty void, and the next minute he shot past, followed by shouts of, "stop that man!"

Arriving breathless at the altar, Jyp came face to face with Mr Benson who regarded him with growing horror.

'I'm not too late, am I?'

'Who the devil are you and how did you get in?'

'It's Jyp - don't you recognise me?'

Benson's nose wrinkled in disgust and stepped back to avoid contact.

'Where's the usher?' He appealed for assistance to the congregation at large and in answer to his prayer two exquisitely attired attendants appeared from nowhere and took up positions either side of Jyp.

'Get this tramp out of here before the bride arrives.'

One of the attendants laid a firm hand on Jyp's arm. 'Excuse me sir, would you mind?'

Jyp couldn't believe this was all happening to him. After all the trouble he had taken to get to the service in time. He made a last gesture. 'But Mr Benson, don't you recognise me, I'm Jyp – you know, Jefferson Patbottom. I'm your Best Man, remember?'

As the reality of the intolerable situation began to sink in, Benson clutched his head.

'I don't believe it! Pratbottom! What do you think this is – some sort of fancy dress party?

Get out of here!'

The bubbles formed on his lips as he tried to pretend it was all a ghastly nightmare. Before he could follow it up with more explicit language that would do full justice to the situation, the organ struck a chord and the far doors swung back to reveal Patience gliding up the aisle towards them on the arm of her elderly parent.

Benson hastily stood in front of Jyp doing his best to hide him from view but it was too late.

Letting go of her father's arm, Patience rushed forward, tripped and clutched at the nearest pew for support as she caught sight of Jyp and began to scream.

On cue, the organist made another attempt at starting the introduction, accompanied by a medley of squeals and juddering sounds from the organ.

Amid the bedlam of protests, with several people fainting in the nearby pews, Benson tried in vain to get Jyp out of sight.

'Is that you, Jyp?' Patience managed a smile of welcome and swayed towards him. 'Where have you been?'

Jyp moistened his lips. 'It wasn't my fault. I got involved in a security exercise.'

He glanced around at the disbelieving faces. 'It's all hush, hush.'

'Hush, hush?' bellowed Benson. 'In that outfit?' He shouldered the ushers aside. 'Let me deal with this.'

He advanced threateningly on Jyp and grabbed him by his lapels. 'There's only one way to deal with people like you.'

Rallying, Patience rushed forward. 'No, don't – he doesn't mean it!'

Pulling himself up to his full height, Benson glared at her. 'Either that worm goes, or I do!'

For a moment they stood facing each other, unwilling to give way. Seeing her chances of marriage slipping away, Patience reached out helplessly. 'I thought you loved me, Howard.'

Unaware of the drama, an elderly vicar made his way to the altar, murmuring to himself. 'What did I do with my hearing aid last night? I knew I put it somewhere. Ah, there we are, that's better.' He adjusted the aid and beamed around. 'Good morning everyone - are we all here?'

His benevolent gaze took in Jyp and his voice faltered. 'I say, your attire is a little unusual for the occasion, don't you think?'

'You can say that again, Vicar,' snorted Benson, turning to Patience. 'I don't know how you came to pick this halfwit in the first place.' He breathed heavily. 'I've long suspected what you were up to together – now I know.'

'How can you say that, Howard?'

But Howard had had enough. 'That's it. I can't waste any more time here, I've got more important things to think about. It's time I got back to my figures.'

'I know what figure you had in mind,' burst out Patience furiously. 'That was the one you swore was your sister!'

Realising what a perilous situation he was getting into Jyp held up his hand, pleading, 'Don't argue over such a trivial matter, at a time like this, I beg you.' He tried to laugh but the sound came out more like a demented croak. 'Remember, this is your wedding day – the happiest day of your life. Look, I'll go, I promise.'

Ignoring his presence Benson drew in his breath for a final broadside. 'I've long suspected that you felt this way and now this proves it. That's it – the wedding off!' And with that, he stalked out.

There was a stunned silence and the Vicar spoke up plaintively, 'Have I missed something? Will the best man produce the ring?'

Jyp started edging out. 'I really think it's time I got back to the office. They'll wonder where I am.'

'Wait!' Patience implored desperately, doing her best to retrieve the hopeless situation. 'They're not the only ones.' She reached out a hand coyly. 'Dear Jefferson, you don't have to pretend with me. I know what it must have meant for you to see me snatched away like this – it must have been dreadful for you - I do understand.'

'I'll be in touch, I promise.' promised Jyp weakly, backing to the entrance.

'Don't leave me – we have so much to look forward to, now that we've come together again.'

'Is that the time, I'll be late.'

Suddenly, Benson was back, snatching up his coat and umbrella. 'I nearly forgot. Cost me a tidy sum this did. Well, I'll see you at the office as usual on Monday, Patience. Don't be late, we've got a lot of figures to catch up on – you know what Head Office is like.'

Furiously, Patience pulled off her ring and threw it at him. 'That's it! I'm not coming back, Howard. I'll go home to Daddy. He'll know how to look after me, won't you, Daddy?'

But Daddy decided he'd had enough, in company with most of the congregation who were already leaving.

'Daddy?' She turned to Jyp. 'Jefferson?'

But she found herself talking to an empty space.

Some hours later, a weary Jyp climbed out of the train completely exhausted, looking forward to changing back into his own clothes again and relaxing with a soothing drink. As he came in sight of the office he noticed a flurry of activity and a shout went up. 'There he is, Officer!'

Bewildered, Jyp looked around at the expectant faces and came face to face with the feared Inspector Grooch who stepped forward importantly and took out his notebook with a flourish.

'Ah, there you are, sir. Did you know there has been a break-in at the shop?' He looked more closely at Jyp's attire and his voice took on a formal tone. 'May I ask where you obtained those items you are wearing, sir, as they fit the description of the said golfing gear stolen from the aforesaid premises?'

Chapter Ten

A Promising Candidate

Aware they were all waiting for an answer Jyp experienced the same guilty feeling he remembered from his schooldays when facing the Head across the desk and being asked for an explanation as to why the prefect had found two jars of raspberry jam in his locker that had gone missing from the tuck shop.

He was about to follow his old school friend's advice by looking squarely in his accuser's face and deny all knowledge of the event when the Inspector's mobile went off and he stepped away with a muttered excuse.

'Yes, who's that? Oh, hello, sir.' He cupped his hand over the mobile and called out sharply. 'Ferris! Oh, there you are – here, take over will you. If there's any monkey business, take him down to the station.' He picked up the mobile again and his voice took on a honey tone, 'Sorry about that, sir…you were saying? No, nothing important - how can I help you?'

He waved the others away and resumed his conversation.

Dutifully, Sergeant Ferris took over and took out his notebook.

Jyp was racking his brains for a convincing excuse when a sweet voice interrupted his scattered wits with an explanation that sounded like music to his ears.

'It's quite all right, Sergeant – we know all about it.'

'You do, Miss?' The sergeant looked relieved and put his notebook away.

'Yes. Jefferson borrowed the clothes with our full permission.'

'Oh, well that's that then, if you say so. I'll be getting on my way, Miss.'

Julie waited until the sergeant was out of sight, then turned to Jyp. 'Where on earth have you been all this time and why did you have to pinch that awful golfing outfit. You'd better come in and explain.'

'Ok.' Jyp followed her back into the office where it was quite plain she expected to have a full and unvarnished account of his behaviour.

'Well?'

'I didn't ask you how your lunch date went,' asked Jyp, stalling for time.

'I had a lovely lunch thank you and your clothes are all pressed and waiting for you to put on. Now, what have you been up to?' Then noticing the state he was in and his woeful expression, she took pity on him and exploded in mirth. 'Oh Jyp, if you could only see yourself – you look like nothing on earth! Wait a minute, your face is positively filthy.'

As she dabbed at his face with a damp cloth, she had an irresistible desire to stroke his cheek that set off an immediate reaction from Jyp. All the hours of pent up frustration and longer swept over him and without thinking he reached out clasped her in his arms and kissed her.

Freeing herself at last, Julie looked up at him reproachfully. 'Why has it taken you so long? I thought you'd forgotten me.' She stroked his cheek again and nestled up.

'I didn't think you'd believe me.' Then in a rush, he burst out, 'I love you, Julie.'

'Oh Jyp, do you really?' She buried her face in his shoulder. 'I thought you'd never get around to it.'

'My aunt keeps telling me that as well,' he said, struck by the co-incidence.

'Now having got that off your chest, what happened – I want to hear all about it. But first you'd better get rid of those smelly old clothes before the boss sees you.'

Five minutes later, Jyp returned looking more presentable, uncertain how to proceed.

'It's a long story,' he began, thinking how idiotic it would sound.

'Well take your time and start at the beginning, you silly man,' she said lovingly. 'There's nobody else around to hear.'

A door opened quietly behind them and Morris peered out, cursing to himself after witnessing the romantic spectacle, and listened intently.

Hearing Jyp unload his tale in faltering bursts, he carefully made a note of Patience's name and left the door ajar so he he could follow the conversion.

'You idiot,' was Julie's verdict. 'Why on earth didn't you tell me about it before – I would have understood. All that business about dressing up in Reg's golfing gear – what a hoot! I'd love to have been there to see it! Did he really go on like that?' She started giggling at the thought. 'What did he say?'

'He was a bit miffed at the outfit I wore and didn't recognise me.'

'I'm not surprised,' Julie tried to keep a straight face. 'Go on.'

'And then when he did he accused Patience of all sorts of things – of being unfaithful and all that sort of thing.' He changed the conversation hastily at the thought, 'and they had a devil of a row. And after all that he expected her to turn up at the office on Monday, he said.'

'No – no wonder she gave him the heave ho – the man's a monster!'

'Yes, and that means she'll be free to chase after me again.' He shuddered at the possibility.

'Well she'll have me to contend with, if she does,' answered Julie stoutly. 'Yes, what is it, Reg?' noticing him hovering in the background.

'Letter for Jyp, Miss - just come in.'

'Oh, no!' groaned Jyp, scanning the writing on the envelope. 'It's Patience - talk of the devil.'

'Well let's see what she says,' encouraged Julie, releasing herself.

Quickly scanning the contents, Jyp clutched his head. 'She wants a job now she's split up.'

'Well, I hope you're not going to be idiotic enough to find her one here.'

'You must be joking,' he said with feeling.

'That's my love. Now what was it we were talking about?' and snuggled up again.

The door closed quietly behind them and soon after Julie's telephone bleeped. She freed herself reluctantly. 'That's his nibs – I'd better answer it.' She listened for a moment and after acknowledging, nodded encouragingly at Jyp. 'It's the boss – he wants to see you right away.'

Stuffing the letter in his pocket, he hurried in.

'Ah Jefferson, take a seat.'

Jyp obeyed and cast an enquiring glance at his new manager. Gone was the affable bearing that was evident on his previous visit. Instead, he was subjected to a curt no nonsense business look that told him that the time for games was over.

'I understand that the exercise I set you was not a particularly overwhelming success,' said Morris nastily, 'largely because all the local traders recognised you. However,' he cut short Jyp's explanations, 'it was a start in the right direction, I suppose. I shall expect a full report. Meanwhile,' he gestured at a pile of files on the desk, 'I have been examining some of the work of my predecessor and see that he had some promising leads that I intend to build on. We don't seem to have done much to make our work known around here and I intend to change all that – expansion is the word. From now on I want us to be known throughout the country for operating a first class security network.'

Taking in the significance of his remarks Jyp had a sinking feeling at what it would all mean to Julie's workload.

'Bearing in mind what this will require from the typing pool,' Morris's voice droned on,

'I have decided to engage another secretary to share the extra burden this will require. I have therefore placed an advertisement in the relevant trade papers and expect some answers soon. No doubt you will wish to assist in the selection.'

Jyp heaved a sigh of relief at the promise of extra help for Julie and nodded his agreement.

'Good, that is all, I think. I'll leave you to get on with your report and perhaps you would let my secretary know about the new arrangements.' Morris concluded his remarks by flexing his hands – a peculiar habit that sparked off a signal in Jyp's mind, but he was so anxious to pass on the latest news that he ignored it.

'At least that means we'll be able to manage this time – not like the chaos old Grimshaw created,' puzzled Julie, hearing the latest news. 'But I wonder what he's planning.'

'Meanwhile, I suppose I'd better knock something out to satisfy our boss,' sighed Jyp moodily.

'Cheer up, darling. Leave it to me, I'm good at trotting out reports like that, after all the school runs we've had.'

* * *

Meanwhile, Morris, their manager, was reflecting on what to do next. If only Simone would get in touch, he brooded. He had come to rely on her advice where women were concerned and her continued silence was unsettling. He flexed his fingers as he always did when facing a problem of this nature. Smoothing his hair back, he glanced in the mirror and was reassured at the sight. He'd never had any problem in the past where his conquests were concerned and he didn't intend to spoil his record. He smirked at the thought. That little girl outside admired his dancing and it was only a matter of time before he had her dancing on a string like all the others. He was on to a good thing where Julie was concerned and nothing must interfere with his plans for her. Meanwhile, the mention of that girl Patience who had designs on Jefferson gave him an idea, and he reached for the phone. Ten minutes later he sat back with a sigh of satisfaction, having told the recruitment agency what he had in mind.

Blissfully unaware of the pitfalls awaiting him, Jyp relaxed and watched Julie lovingly as she made out a report for him, admiring the brisk and professional way she went about her task. At last she was finished and passed it to him for approval.

Glancing up after reading the last page he gave a thumbs up. 'This is great – just what we need. I'd never have managed without your help, darling. Bless you.'

Smiling happily at the compliment, she swivelled on her seat. 'Does that mean I get a kiss?'

Bounding across, Jyp gathered her up in his arms and gave her a hug.

At the sound of the intercom buzzing, Julie broke free reluctantly. 'That's me, I must go, love. He's got a load of dictation he wants me to share with this new girl when she arrives. I'd better find out what he wants.'

'That reminds me,' said Jyp. 'I promised Aunt Cis I'd give her the latest lowdown on our new boss. I'll tell you all about it tomorrow.'

'Don't forget, love – oh, that's him again. Can't stop,' and gathering up her notebook she shot past.

* * *

When he got home his aunt was nowhere to be seen. Finally, after waiting half an hour and looking at his watch and getting peckish, she appeared looking very flustered.

'Don't tell me, I know – I'm awfully sorry, Jyp. I got stuck in a queue and thought I'd never get away. Now sit down while I knock up a quick supper and tell me all about this new boss of yours.'

Trying not to look too closely at the somewhat shrivelled helping of bacon and eggs he was offered, Jyp swallowed them down and did his best to describe the new manager and his habits.

'Hmm, Charles Morris – that name sounds familiar somehow. Give me a few minutes while I think.' Noticing his empty plate, she apologised. 'I'm sorry, love, I'll get you something better for supper tomorrow. Now where was I?'

'Morris,' prompted Jyp, shutting his mind off from the thought of food. 'You thought you might know him.'

'Yes,' her mind strayed. 'If he's the one I think it might be, he was always after the girls.

'Randy Andy' they used to call him, couldn't keep his hands off them. His second name was Andrew,' she explained. She thought back. 'And there was something else about him, if I remember rightly. Rumours were going around that he was a bit of a dodgy character – not just women, but there were talks about him being involved in some sort of blackmail racket, or something like that.'

The news did little to reassure Jyp, as he recalled Morris taking Julie out for lunch and looking very possessive about her.

'How can we find out?' he asked abruptly. 'Is there anyone you know who could give us a clue? There must be someone who knew him.'

'What about that woman Simone you were telling me about?'

He shuddered. 'Don't remind me. She's the last one I want to see again.'

'Well remind me what he looks like. How would you describe him?'

'Well, I suppose he's goodlooking in a slinky sort of way,' he admitted reluctantly. 'The sort women always seem to fall for.'

'I tell you what,' she eyed him encouragingly. 'If you could get a photo of him I'd have a much better idea. Any other habits or mannerisms you can think of?'

Jyp recalled his habit of flexing his fingers but it didn't ring a bell.

'Well, I must love you and leave you, Jyp, I've got a WI meeting this evening and can't afford to miss it, so off you go, shoo.' As she showed him out, she thought of something, 'Oh, by the way, see if you can get a specimen of his writing so we can see if it matches up with that scrap of paper you showed me.'

* * *

Feeling unsatisfied with what he had learnt and still hungry, Jyp's temper was not improved when he encountered an excited Julie at the office the next morning, brimming over with her account of the sumptuous treat she had with their boss. 'He kept me so long over that dictation he took me out to a gorgeous spread to make up for it – you should have been there.' she broke off, 'I'm sorry, I was forgetting, how did you get on?'

'Ok,' he mumbled, doing his best to dismiss the picture of his own meagre fare.

'Well, what did your auntie say? You said she was in the same line of business – did she know him?'

Jyp prudently left out the description his aunt had come up with in case it didn't go down well and temporised. 'She said she would have a better idea if we could get her a photo of him.'

Julie sounded dubious. 'I know Reg has a camera but I don't see how we can get him to pose. He's such a busy man and so good looking. And very charming with it. You ought to have seen him at supper.' She sighed at the memory and Jyp suddenly felt a prickle of jealousy.

So he left it at that, intending to consult Reg at the first opportunity.

The next moment their manager appeared at his door and his announcement drove the thought right out of his head.

'I thought you might like to know that the agency has just been on the phone with a promising candidate and they're sending her along first thing tomorrow. So I want both of you to be here to meet her. And now I must go – I have an urgent appointment. Tomorrow then.'

His news left them with mixed feelings. Julie was delighted and said so. 'My goodness, that was quick. How about that for speed? I can't wait to see how she is, can't you?'

Jyp was non-committal, but couldn't help wondering how Morris had managed to receive a call without it going through the switchboard.

* * *

It wasn't until the following morning that Jyp's suspicions turned out to be fully justified.

If Morris had ever nursed any ambitions to be a circus impresario he would have been snapped up on the spot judging by his performance as he introduced their new secretary.

His announcement wouldn't have been more effective if he had ushered in a parade of jugglers accompanied by a roll of drums. After inviting them all into his office, he threw open his inner door with a theatrical flourish to reveal the excited figure of... Patience.

Before Jyp could recover from the shock she bounded into the room and threw her arms around his neck and gave him a smacking great kiss, much to his embarrassment.

'Oh, Jefferson, how sweet of you to think about me when you knew I needed a job. I can't thank you enough, after all you've done for me.'

Pulling himself free Jyp hotly denied being responsible but the damage was done.

Satisfied from the cold look of disbelief on Julie's face, Morris gave himself a pat on the back at the result he had achieved and with a bland smile suggested they should leave the two young friends to celebrate their reunion in private.

With a crafty look of triumph he followed Julie as she swept from the room, assuring her of his devotion and remarking what an extraordinary coincidence it was that had brought the two young people together again.

The only other person he had overlooked was Reg who for some reason seemed totally absorbed in the new arrival.

Grabbing Jyp's arm as the latter managed to tear himself free and tottered from the office, Reg sighed and mumbled something that barely percolated into his hearing and had to be repeated several times before he could be understood.

'Whass that?'

'I said - what a corker.'

Jyp blinked and attempted to follow his friend's meaning. 'You mean Julie? She's just left.'

'No, that young peach of a woman over there,' pointing shyly at Patience who was smiling dreamily to herself in the corner.

Jyp's jaw dropped in total disbelief. 'You don't mean,' he croaked, 'Patience?'

'Yes – you don't mind?'

'Mind? Why should I mind?' Jyp was even more confused, still grappling with the idea that anyone would consider Patience as being, as his friend put it, "a corker".

'I mean, about,' Reg nodded his head meaningly at the door. 'you know, Julie.'

Jyp's head cleared. 'Mind? Of course I don't mind, Reg. But-but, are you sure we're talking about the same one – Patience, the new secretary?'

'Oh, yes.' Reg's eyes took on a dreamy expression as he goggled at the object of his worship.

Catching his adoring glance for the first time, Patience fluttered her eyelashes demurely and acknowledged his presence with a discreet wave of her hand.

Interpreting her signal as an invitation, Reg caught his breath. He clutched Jyp's arm.

'I say, do you think it awfully forward of me if I took a photo of her?'

Jyp was about to say - not a chance with old Morris keeping an eye on her – when a sudden thought struck him as he remembered his aunt's request, leaving him weak with gratitude at the unexpected opportunity it presented. He swallowed and nursed Reg's shoulder affectionately. 'I've got an even better idea - why don't you take one of her taking dictation from Morris in his office – he'd be delighted to add it to the office collection to,' his mind searched wildly for a possible reason and a plausible solution suddenly occurred to him. 'I know, to celebrate his new expansion plans, of course. And while you're at it, don't forget to get a good shot of his face to go with it – that will please him no end.'

Leaving Reg still repeating his thanks, Jyp hurried back to explain the new turn of events, realising in advance what an uphill task it was likely to be after she had witnessed his recent embrace.

'With who?' was all she said after listening to his recital. Disregarding the fact that she should have said 'whom', we can only draw a blind on her subsequent comments on the situation, leaving him in no doubt as to her attitude about the whole affair, after being influenced by a certain wily manager who was celebrating his success by treating himself to an extra large cigar in the cafe next door.

'Are you seriously trying to tell me that Reg is suddenly infatuated with your Patience?' she said coldly. 'I thought she only has eyes for you?'

'She didn't mean it,' he pleaded desperately. 'You heard what she said, she was only expressing her gratitude.'

'That's not what it looked like where I was standing.'

Feeling more like a shipwrecked sailor seeing the rescue ship disappearing over the horizon, Jyp persevered against what seemed like hopeless odds.

'But I had nothing to do with her appointment – it was Morris who chose her.'

'Really.' Her bottled up fury boiled over. 'That's not what Charles told me – he said you begged him to take her on.'

Her statement took his breath away. 'That's not true!' he denied vehemently. 'He's lying.

She's the last person I would have chosen. Don't you know by now that you're the only one I want in my life? I love you!'

His outburst was so unexpected Julie was stirred by his passion and started to weaken.

'But why should he say things like that if it wasn't true?'

'Because,' his aunt's warning trembled on his lips, and before he could stop himself he went on blindly. 'because he wants to add you to his list of conquests. Aunt Cis told me all about him – she says he's a womaniser. Everyone knows what he's like.'

'How can she know – she's never met him.' Even as she said it, Julie was shaken by the news.

Jyp hesitated, then confessed sheepishly. 'Aunt Cis asked me to get hold of a photo to make sure. When Reg asked me if he could take a picture of Patience I realised it was a heaven sent opportunity. I told him to make sure he got Morris in the picture as well so I could show it to her.'

Julie tried to look stern but failed. 'Poor Reg – you didn't tell him what he was letting himself in for.'

'No,' Jyp admitted. 'I don't think he would have believed me anyway – he's not the only one,' he added, glancing at her hopefully.

'I give up. You men are all the same. Oh, goodness, is that the time?' Glancing at her watch, she exclaimed horrified. 'I'm late for an appointment with Dad's solicitors.'

'Nothing serious, I hope?' Jyp asked sympathetically, helping her on with her coat.

'No, Dad's all right – he asked me to go along on his behalf. It's my grandad. He passed away recently.' Her face looked sad and she dashed away a tear. 'He was so full of life – I never thought he would go like that, tripping over Ben, his lovely old spaniel. I wonder what will become of him – I'd love to keep Ben myself now, if that's possible.'

'Is there anything I can do?' added Jyp awkwardly.

A brief half forgiving smile flitted across her face. 'No, just stay out of mischief. I'll tell you about it when I get back.' She leaned forward and gave him a kiss just as Morris let himself in and heard the tail end of their conversation.

'Ah, Julie, you off then? I was just going to get you to finish off that dictation of ours. Never mind, I'll get young Patience to do it – give her some practice. Why don't you join us Jefferson and see how your friend is getting on? No doubt you will want to see she gets home safely when we've finished, as you are old friends,' he repeated, to rub it in.

The front door slammed behind Julie, cutting off his remarks as he ushered them in.

Before long the warmth of the office and the drone of Morris's voice caused Jyp to start nodding off and it wasn't until he realised that he was being asked a question that he abruptly woke up with a start. 'Don't you agree with me, Jefferson.'

'Eh, of course, sir.'

'Good, well I think that's all, Miss... er... Patience. If you get that lot typed up, we'll, yes, who's that?'

'Excuse me, sir.' Reg's face appeared at the door, raising his smartphone hopefully.

'Yes, what is it?'

'I was just wondering if I might take a picture of our new team. Purely for our own records,' he added hurriedly, noting the forbidding look on Morris's face. 'And to celebrate our new plans for expansion under such a celebrated leader.' He bowed ingratiatingly at Morris. Jyp gave him a warning glance, telling him not to overdo it.

Just as Morris was about to say 'No' Patience squealed her delight. 'Oh, that would be lovely – I can keep it to remind me of my first day here.'

'Actually,' said Jyp deferentially. 'It would be quite a good idea to show our people in Whitehall – they're always looking for something to celebrate.'

Morris rustled his papers impatiently. 'Ok, but hurry up, don't take all day - and keep me out of it.'

After the meeting Jyp steered Reg aside and had a quick look at his efforts, noting with glee that despite Morris's instructions they managed to get most of him in. 'Just what we need,' he summed up. 'Excellent.'

'Do you think I've done her justice?' asked Reg eagerly.

'You couldn't have done better,' Jyp nodded his approval as he scanned the images, his attention fixed on shots of Morris. He hesitated, 'There's only one snag – how soon can we get any copies?'

Reg nudged him with a grin. 'Terrific, isn't she. You can't fool me – I know, you want some of Patience as well.'

'No,' Jyp was quite definite. 'It's Morris we want.'

'Why's that? I didn't know you were his fan, particularly after that run around he gave you the other day.'

Making sure they were not overheard Jyp started to explain, then changed his mind. 'Can't go into it just now. Tell you what,' as he remembered the laptop he'd noticed at his aunt's, 'leave this with me overnight and I'll knock off any copies you need at the same time.'

Reg heaved a sigh. 'I don't like to part with it, but seeing it's you…let me have half a dozen of the best shots of her and it's a deal.'

They shook hands solemnly and Reg passed his smartphone over. 'Don't lose it, I may never get another chance, knowing old Morris.'

'You can trust me.'

'Right, I'll leave you to it before he changes his mind. Look out,' as the door began to open behind them. 'See you.'

'Just a minute,' Morris called out quickly as Reg disappeared from view. 'Was that Reg, I want to have a word with him.'

'I'm afraid you've missed him,' Jyp lied cheerfully. 'He left five minutes ago – that was the postman.'

'Blast the man, it's not clocking off time yet.'

'I think he said something about a sick relative,' said Jyp hastily. 'He's usually very good with the hours he puts in.'

'Well, tell him I want him in my office first thing tomorrow – I take it you've got something to occupy your time meanwhile.'

'Of course, sir,' agreed Jyp hastily, hiding the smartphone behind his back.

'Hmm. Well don't let me keep you.' He watched suspiciously as Jyp retreated into the office, changing the smartphone from one hand to the other as he saluted and waved with each hand in turn.

Chapter Eleven

In the Money

When he got home bursting with news about his success he found his aunt full of apologies.

'You must be starving. Now sit down, I've got a delicious supper for you all ready to make up for that awful scratch meal you had to endure yesterday.

'But Aunt, I've got just the info you've been asking for.'

'Not another word, otherwise it will all spoil. You can tell me afterwards when you've got this lot inside you.' And so saying she slapped down a steaming plate in front of him, full of enticing smells that drove all thoughts of his latest coup out of his head.

As he finally wiped his mouth and pushed back his chair with a satisfied sigh, she whisked away his plate.

'Now, let's see what you were trying to tell me.'

With a flourish, Jyp whipped out Reg's smartphone. 'Ta-ra!'

Unimpressed, Auntie Cis took it from him gingerly. 'What am I supposed to do with this?'

'It's full of shots of you-know-who, that's what!'

'You mean Morris - how did you manage that?'

Jyp allowed a note of cautious optimism to creep into his voice. 'It turned out that Reg at the office was so keen to get some pictures of Patience that he jumped at the chance of taking some shots of her.' A grin broke out. 'So I made sure he included Morris as well.'

'That's a crafty one – I can see I'll have to watch you in future,' she smiled her approval.

'I know it wasn't very sporting but it was the only way I could think of getting it done without too much suspicion. As it was,' he reflected, 'I've got a feeling that old Morris tumbled to it afterwards – but it was too late to do anything about it.'

'Well don't let's worry too much about that. The main thing is that you've got the pics we were after. Now all we need to know is how to unload the pictures and work out how many we need. All this modern technology is beyond me.'

'That's easy, Aunt.' He waved the smartphone at her. 'Just think of this as a miniature computer – that's all it is. Now,' he fed some instructions into it, 'all I need to do is to transfer the images onto your laptop and voila – it's all done.'

'That's amazing. Now what?'

'Now we can see what the shots look like and decide which ones we want to print out. Here we are.'

As the images came up on the screen Aunt Cis pointed excitedly. 'That's him – I'd know that face anywhere. Well done, Jyp. Wait a minute, we'd better not leave those shots of Morris on there. If he catches sight of them he'll do a runner.'

'I've already thought of that.' He pressed a button on the printer. 'There you are, that's the shot of Morris we want, now for a bit of touching up.' He did some quick cropping. 'That takes care of him.'

'How did you do that – he's disappeared.'

'That's the idea. Now all we need is to run off some copies for Reg.'

He set a number on the printer and pressed a button. 'Hey presto, I didn't need to count the copies, did I – it does it all for you.'

'Excellent,' his aunt said sweetly. 'Now there's only one thing left to do.'

Jyp groaned. 'I thought we'd got everything we needed – now what?'

Aunt Cis favoured him with an encouraging beam and patted him on the back. 'All we need now is a set of his fingerprints.'

'What do you want those for?'

His aunt looked at him in surprise. 'To check if he's committed any offence under another name of course, silly boy. I would have thought that was obvious. Knowing that character, he probably operated under half a dozen aliases by now.'

'Does that mean I've got to go through this all over again?' Jyp was horrified.

'How on earth do I do that?'

His aunt made some soothing noises. 'All you have to do is to bring me a piece of paper he's been handling and leave the rest to me. But make sure you don't let your own prints get plastered all over it.'

'That's great.' Jyp heaved himself out of his seat with a sigh. 'Glad to know it's nothing too strenuous.'

'Good, I'm glad we've sorted that out. Now, have we got enough copies of this Patience of yours?'

Jyp winced. 'She's not my Patience anymore, with a bit of luck, Aunt. We've got half a dozen here – that should be enough to keep Reg happy. Is there anything I've forgotten?'

'No, you've done brilliantly. Why don't you have an early night – you look as if you could do with it.'

'Thanks, I think I might.' He glanced at the prints in his hand. 'He'll be jumping up and down with delight when he sees this, if I know him.'

* * *

As it turned out, Reg was in no condition to jump up and down when he hobbled in next morning. At first sight it looked as if he had been dragged through a hedge backwards. In fact, he was in such a mess that Jyp hardly recognised him. One eye was swollen, he had an arm in a sling and the other was relying on a crutch to get him through the doorway.

'What on earth?' Jyp helped him weave his way to the nearest chair. 'What happened to you?'

'You may well ask,' Reg panted, subsiding with a thump. 'I was just turning the corner down the road when some lunatic drove straight at me and the next minute I was flying through the air and landed on his bonnet.'

'Here, take it easy.' Jyp help him straighten up. 'Was he drunk or something?'

Reg snorted. 'Drunk, my eye. When I came to, he was rifling through my pockets – told me some tale about looking for my driving licence to see who I was. He couldn't wait, could he?'

Jyp had a sudden guilty premonition and fished out the smartphone. 'It wasn't this he was after, was it?'

With a weary gesture, Reg took it. 'Ah thanks. I doubt it, he was probably looking for money, he didn't stop to tell me. By the way, did you have any luck with the pics?'

'Of course, here you are. Are these any good?'

Reg thumbed through the prints and eyed them reverently. 'She's gorgeous, isn't she.'

Jyp coughed and tried not to shudder. 'Yes, great – how are you feeling?'

'Oh, some kind old boy phoned up for an ambulance and they patched me up. They wanted to whisk me off to the hospital but I couldn't wait to get back.' He gazed at the photos longingly. 'Can't wait to see her face.'

'Someone talking about me?' A voice cooed in his ear, 'Oh Reg, what have they done to you?' After hearing the explanations, she gazed in rapture at the pictures and turned to Reg again. 'How wonderful – is that really me?' Without waiting for an answer she smothered him with kisses. 'Oh you poor dear – you did this just for me?'

Recovering with a blissful smile, Reg put the record straight. 'I only took the shots – it was Jyp who went to all the trouble of getting the prints.'

Before he could finish Patience swayed across and planted a smacking kiss on his face in turn to make sure he was not forgotten, just as Julie entered.

'What is it with you?' she wailed, as soon as they found themselves alone. 'I've only got to leave the office for five minutes before you're at it again.'

'But Julie, I can explain.'

'It had better be good, is all I can say. So, what's the excuse this time?'

Jyp took a deep breath, wondering where to start. He marshalled his facts and lowered his voice, after having a quick look around. 'Well, you know how potty Reg is about Patience.'

Julie drummed her fingers on the desk. 'He's not the only one, it appears.'

'That's not true.' Jyp cleared his throat and tried again. 'It all began when I persuaded Reg to take a picture of Patience in Morris's office, so as I could include a shot of him as well.'

'Why did you want a shot of Morris?'

'I told you. Aunt Cis wanted one because she was sure,' he hesitated, 'that it was someone she knew who she suspected of being a 'ladykiller'.'

'Like someone else I could mention,' interrupted Julie coldly.

'Well anyway, I persuaded Reg to let me have his smartphone and ran some copies off at home so that Reg could have the copies he wanted and at the same time I managed to run off a copy of Morris for Aunt Cis.'

'How did that help?'

Jyp moistened his lips. 'Aunt Cis recognised him right away and wants me to, well never mind what she wants. The upshot was that Morris thought Reg might have an incriminating shot that might do him some damage and tried to get hold of it last night before Reg left.' He paused to let this sink in and went on, 'The next thing poor old Reg gets run over outside the office this morning on his way in and someone went through his pockets. You can guess the rest.'

Julie bridled. 'Are you trying to say Charles was responsible for that? I don't believe it - you must be crazy. I know what it is, you're jealous! He's always been kind and considerate.' Fortified by her diagnosis, she felt more reassured and was almost inclined to forget the whole matter and put it down to office gossip.

'Please yourself,' said Jyp shortly. 'Ask Reg yourself.'

'I can't believe it. Where is Reg, I must see how he is, poor man.'

'He's not a pretty sight,' warned Jyp awkwardly. 'I think Patience is in with him now. I can't see him being fit enough to do anything at the moment in his condition. I expect she's ordering a cab to get him home.'

'Good for her. Anyway,' she fired a parting shot, 'you'll be pleased to hear that I won't have to listen to any more of your silly office feuding much longer. As soon as I've seen Reg, I'm going to see Charles about giving in my notice.'

'But why – is it something I've said?' said Jyp, bewildered, but the sound of the door slamming behind her was the only response he received. Taken aback at her sudden announcement, he was left in a dazed state. He pottered around in the office, picking up papers and putting them down again aimlessly, trying to make sense of her decision and wondering what on earth he could do to put things right between them again.

Meanwhile later that afternoon, behind the closed door in his private office, Morris was hugging himself at the amazing good news he had just been told in confidence by Julie, mixed with a deep sense of frustration that he had nobody he could trust to share it with, when the phone rang.

'Is that you, Charles?'

Tingling with excitement, Morris instantly recognised those honey tones he'd almost given up hearing again.

'Simone? Is that you – where have you been? I've been looking for you everywhere.'

'I've missed you too, Charles,' came her mournful reply. 'Ever since that awful business at the hotel, the Embassy practically disowned me. They treated me like a, how you say, chittel.'

'Chattel,' he corrected automatically. 'Never mind that - what happened?'

'I'm a telling you, darleeng. Just because I mistook that old bore, the Brigadier, for Jeep, they packed me off to some ghastly place in outer Mongolia or somewhere...I thought my last hour had come.'

'Wait a minute, what was that you said about Jyp?'

'I thought you knew – the manager was awfully stuffy. I never thought I'd hear the last about it, you'd have thought I'd commited some crime, carting me off like that. I was distraught, darling, and you ought to have heard what the Brigadier's wife called me.'

'Never mind what the manager said.'

'You should have been there – where were you. I was lost without you.'

'Yes, yes, but what about Jyp? Did you do what I told you?'

A coy laugh floated down the phone. 'But darling, you know I always do what you tell me.'

Morris tried to keep a note of eagerness out of his voice. 'Did you see him after I left you?'

'Of course, silly man. He called on me thinking it was the Gents and I persuaded him to stay.'

'And then? What happened?' His voice sharpened.'You didn't let him get away?'

A husky whisper was all he could hear at first, then a gurgle.

'What was that?' Are you still there?'

'I was just thinking. He was so shy, silly man. He was thinking all kinds of excuses to get away when he found out.'

'Found out – what?' he almost shouted.

'Well we were, how you say, in the all together.'

He let out a sigh of pent up relief. 'Are you saying he was in bed with you?'

'Of course.' Her answer held a note of reproof. 'I have not lost my touch, as he found out.'

'Listen Simone, this is important. Will you send me an email, giving me all the details – and make sure you don't leave anything out.'

'You know I'd do anything for you, darling. And what is your news – I am longing to hear all about you and what you have been doing – you naughty boy.'

'You're not going to believe this, Simone, but we're on to a chance of a lifetime.' He lowered his voice guardedly in case anyone was listening. 'That young secretary of mine I was telling you about.'

'Julie?' her voice sounded reproachful. 'I thought you promised to keep away from her, after all those other girls you told me about.'

'It's nothing like that,' he hastened to assure her. 'It's purely business this time.'

'That's what you told me last time,' she reminded him. 'And the time before.'

'No, this is strictly on the up and up,' he promised fervently. 'You know you're the only one, as far as I'm concerned. You always were,' he added quickly to forestall any more details of his past history coming to light. 'Listen, this is a whammy of all whammies. Get a load of this,' he eased himself into a more comfortable position. 'This Julie has just come back from her old solicitor on account of her granddad snuffing it, and wait for it, she's been left a packet!'

'Wow!' she interrupted catching on, 'and you're going to help her invest it.'

'Hold your horses, we've got to take this easy, one step at a time,' he cautioned her. 'She's feeling upset about the old boy, seeing he was her favourite, so we've got to tread a bit wary. She's looking for someone she can trust and help her get over it, so yours truly is going to be there for a shoulder to lean on.'

'I get you, softly softly approach – you were always good at that, lover boy.'

He smirked and ran a hand through his hair. 'Meanwhile, get that email off to me right away. I need it to silence that brat Jyp who's treading on my heels – I think he fancies himself in that department and I need to put a stop to it, pronto.'

'Will do, I'm tapping it out right now.'

'And don't forget to put in all the naughty bits – hot it up, you know the sort of thing.'

'I've got you, lover boy. Leave it to me.' Her slinky voice rose to a squeak. 'Jeepers, who'd have thought we'd get this far with that spying lark.'

'Steady on,' he looked around furtively. 'You never know who might be listening – we might be bugged.'

'Are you kidding? Don't tell me you haven't thought about that. Yessir, we're onto a goldmine at last. All those years of fooling those security nuts has paid off – we're in the money at last, lover boy.'

'Well, don't count your chickens yet. You get that email off and I'll get ready to break the news to Julie – that should put paid to that meddlesome office boy. I can't wait to hear what she says.'

* * *

Blissfully ignorant, Julie and Jyp carried on their normal duties unaware of the dark clouds gathering over their heads.

In a side room, Julie was shocked by the effects of the accident that had left its mark on Reg and was relieved at the sight of a blossoming relationship that was taking place before her eyes. It was immediately obvious that he was enjoying his reunion with Patience - who up to that point she had regarded with deep suspicions as a rival for the affections of Jyp. In fact, there existed such a cosy atmosphere of loving care between the two that she became completely disarmed by the spectacle of Patience who was embracing the invalid with loving care.

'Oh, I do apologise for breaking in like this but I heard all about it from Jyp and I had to see for myself. You poor thing, what have they done to you?'

Disentangling himself with difficulty, Reg smiled contentedly. 'Never mind what that idiot of a driver did, he brought us together and that's all I ever wanted, eh darling?'

Smoothing his face, Patience snuggled up closer. 'Oh yes, I never realised how much I cared before that happened to my poor sweetheart.' She sighed. 'I think it was those beautiful photos that were responsible.

They were so lovely – thank you darling. I didn't know you were such a clever photographer.'

'To be fair,' admitted Reg, 'if it wasn't for Jyp getting those prints done at home we would have been up the creek. That thieving nurk who crashed into me might have pinched the lot if he'd had the chance.' He looked up at Julie. 'I expect Jyp told you all about him going through all my pockets.'

Hearing his unvarnished account of the incident, Julie experienced a feeling of guilt at having disbelieved Jyp in the first place and promised herself that she would make up for it somehow. Feeling more cheered at the prospect, Julie leaned over and patted Reg's hand. 'I'm so glad you're feeling better, Reg. Now you must promise me to take it easy. I'll have a word with Mr Morris to make sure you have some time off to get over it.'

With their thanks ringing in her ears, Julie set out to look for Jyp to apologise for her behaviour. She came across him just as he was searching though her dictation, trying to find an example of Morris's dictation without success.

Seeing her, he quickly dropped the papers on the desk, hoping he hadn't been observed but Julie was so preoccupied in deciding the best way to approach him she didn't appear to notice.

'There you are, darling.' She smiled tentatively, running a hand down his arm. Then deciding to take the bull by the horns, she looked up at him appealingly. 'I was awfully mean not to trust you. Have you forgiven me?'

Blinking at the sudden change of heart Jyp hurriedly reassured her, 'Don't give it another thought.'

She swayed towards him. 'Does that mean I get a kiss?'

Jyp brightened up like a Roman candle on fireworks night. Suiting action to words, he clasped her in his arms and gave her a long and lingering kiss. 'Like that?'

'Mmm. I'm so glad we're together again, darling.' She became practical. 'Now that we've got that sorted, I've got so much to tell you about that wonderful Granddad of mine.' She brushed away a tear. 'You'll never guess what he's done.'

He smiled indulgently and hazarded a wild guess at random. 'He's left you his Teddy Bear set?'

'No,' he's left me a collection of rings and things that have been handed down through the family since the year dot. I can't believe it. I don't know how much they're worth but it means we won't have to worry about money for simply ages. What do you think of that?' She trembled with excitement at the thought.

He said nothing and after a while let her go.

'Well, what do you think? No more worrying about looking for spies and bogymen.' She glanced up at him again breathlessly, waiting for his approval.

Jyp stirred uneasily. 'I'll have to think about it. I've never had to rely on anyone else before.'

'But it's me, silly – just the two of us, nobody else.' She broke off. 'Oh, that sounds like his nibs, shan't be a tick.'

Five minutes later she was back, her face set and pale. 'Have you seen this?' waving an email at him.

His mind still grappling with what the future would mean to both of them, he answered distractedly, 'No, what is it?'

At that moment he caught sight of her face and was alarmed at the change. Gone was her air of contentment and certainty about the future. Her mind that previously was full of rosy thoughts was banished in an instant and in its place a searing look of fury that was enough to shrivel him on the spot.

'Now I understand why you didn't want to get tied down when you had that tart waiting in the wings. How could you!' And she burst into tears.

Jyp regarded her helplessly. 'What are you talking about? There's no one else as far as I'm concerned – there never was.'

'Well how do you account for this?' She brandished the email at him furiously.

'I don't know what you're on about.'

Julie smouldered as she read out an extract. 'How I long to have you back in bed again after our night of passion!' She glanced down the page, 'And guess who it's signed by – Simone, remember her?'

Jyp gulped and stammered. 'It wasn't like that – you've got it all wrong.'

'So you admit you were in bed with her?' Julie threw the email at him scornfully. 'You'd better see what else she said, in case you've forgotten.'

Picking it up gingerly he held it at arms length and read it as if it was about to go off in his face. Collecting his wits, he shook with disbelief at the words. 'It's all lies. Listen, if you want the truth I admit landing up in bed with her.'

'That's all I want to know,' she cried, pushing him away. 'You've been pretending to love me and all the time you've been carrying on with this...' the words failed her.

He gripped her arm. 'You don't understand, I wandered into her room by mistake looking for the bathroom and she slipped me a mickey finn, and when I woke up she did her best to get me to stay.'

'So of course you refused,' she finished for him contemptuously. 'A likely story.'

'It's true!' he persisted vehemently. 'I give you my word – don't you see, it's all Morris's doing, trying to split us up.'

'So, now it's all Charles's fault now, is it? Well, that's it, as far as I'm concerned. You can have your floosy and do what you like with her. I've finished with you and I never want to see you again!' With that she burst into tears and stormed out of the room.

Chapter Twelve

An Iceberg on Wheels

As the day wore on the atmosphere in the office became more and more gloomy. Julie was walking around stiffly, not talking to anyone; Jyp had long given up trying to get an answer out of her after several frigid encounters; and Reg was still resisting Patience's efforts to go home and rest while he did his best to intercede on Jyp's behalf, without success.

In short, if anyone had had the temerity to call in for any reason, they would have been met with such a blank response they might have thought they had wandered into some sort of secret service headquarters.

While he was brooding on Julie's mistaken attitude and the injustice of it all, mingled with remorse that he had not come clean with her earlier, he was left with wondering how on earth he could get hold of the information his aunt had so sorely needed and relied on him to provide. If he could somehow prove once and for all what a crook Morris really was, it might make all the difference and help to go some way to repairing the icy relationship that had developed between him and Julie. Not that it would make much difference to their future together now that she had come into all that money, he reflected moodily. He had to admit that even if they managed to get together again, the thought of having to be dependent on her wealth hit his pride where it hurt and went against all his lifetime beliefs that the man should be the sole breadwinner in the family.

His unhappy state of mind was interrupted by the appearance of Patience who was beckoning him from the door. Taking a hurried look around to make sure Julie was not around and find something else to accuse him of, he quickly joined her.

'What is it – Reg all right?' he asked anxiously.

'Yes, he's fine. He's just finding it too much after that accident, so I'm taking him home. Is there anything you want to see him about before we go?'

'Yes, tell him —' At the last minute he fought back the words that sprang to mind, and decided events were complicated enough as it was without bringing Patience into it. 'I'll come and have a word.' he temporised.

'So you see, Reg,' he finished his account lamely, 'it's all getting rather difficult.'

'Difficult? I don't know what you're beefing about.' Reg scratched his head wonderingly. 'Let's get this straight. Julie has suddenly come into all this money and this is a problem? Mate, if I were in your shoes I'd be laughing my head off – not going around looking like a lost cow. I mean to say, I ask you.'

'Well, I see things differently.' Jyp remained stubbornly morose.

'Now if that Morris bloke hears about it, he'll be all over her,' reflected Reg. 'If I were you, I'd put in a few words in that direction.'

'It's no good, she'll never listen to me now after that Simone episode.' Jyp heaved a sigh.

'She's just an iceberg on wheels. I might just as well not exist, and as for Morris, I don't think he cares for me over much. In fact, I have a nasty feeling...'

Their heart to heart was interrupted by Patience hovering in the background, looking on anxiously, like a mother hen defending her chick. 'Now don't you get my Reg worked up – can't you see he's still an invalid and needs looking after. In fact, it's time I took you home and have a proper rest, Reg dear. You don't mind, Jefferson?'

'No, no, you're quite right.' He stepped back and waved them off. 'Off you go, Reg and make sure you get some rest, and if I'm not around for any reason when you get back,' he hesitated, 'keep an eye on things and make sure she's ok.'

'No troubles,' waved Reg as he was wheeled away. 'Leave it to me.'

Feeling reassured Jyp turned and immediately came face to face with Julie.

There was an awkward pause. Jyp made an attempt to fill the gap. 'You've just missed Reg, he's gone home. Anything I can do?'

'You've done quite enough, thank you,' she remarked coldly. 'I'm going out to lunch with Charles – someone I can trust.'

Still smarting from her change in attitude, Jyp turned to leave dejectedly then stopped, his mind working furiously. If Morris was taking her out for lunch it gave him the opportunity he was waiting for. He returned to the office and listened until he heard a murmur of voices then the sound of a door closing.

After a few minutes, he counted up to twenty and ventured forth. To make sure, he tapped at Morris's door and waited, his nerves jumping, then opened the door and went in. The room was empty. Without wasting any further time, he searched the desk for the information he was seeking. He was about to give up when he caught sight of a half torn scrap of paper poking out from under a pile of correspondence. He snatched at it and perused it eagerly. It was a short handwritten note to Julie signed by Charles. His heart leapt – just what he wanted.

Just as he was carefully stowing it away, folded between two other sheets to avoid leaving any fingerprints the door suddenly opened and in walked Morris.

'What are you doing?'

The voice came out of the blue, the last voice he was expecting. Jumping back nervously Jyp stammered, 'Just tidying up to save you time.'

'Thank you, I can take care of that,' snapped Morris, glancing around suspiciously. Then feeling an explanation was necessary. 'Forgot my wallet.' Picking it up he flipped it open to check the contents were still there. Satisfied, he slipped it back in his pocket and stared hard at Jyp. 'No need for you to wait – Julie will see to things when we get back.' As if adding emphasis, he flexed his fingers triggering off a familiar chord in Jyp's memory.

'No, of course.' Jyp backed hurriedly to the door, content with the knowledge that he had secured what he was looking for, leaving Morris filled with the knowledge that something needed to be done to get rid of the growing problem Jyp presented.

Once outside, Jyp wiped his forehead. Satisfied to see Patience had returned and was able to hold the fort he rushed away, intent on getting his evidence back to Aunt Cis and in his hurry scarcely noticing Julie as she waited in the entrance.

Luckily for him, it was not one of his aunt's bridge party days and she pounced on the evidence he produced with eagerness. 'You sure you haven't touched this?' she queried, as she stored the paper carefully in tissue paper. 'Good,' she nodded satisfied at his thumbs up. 'Now all we need to do is to have this checked up – anything else?' She noticed his slight hesitation and waited.

'There is something that keeps nagging at me. Ah yes,' he remembered, 'he has this peculiar habit of flexing his knuckles, like this,' he demonstrated by linking his hands together. As his memory came back, he snapped his fingers. 'That's it! I knew there was something odd about it – his middle finger has a white band on it, as if...'

'He should be wearing a wedding ring!' exclaimed his aunt triumphantly. 'Well done.

Of course,' she added trying to be fair, 'it could mean he's divorced – but if your Julie knew this, it would certainly be a turn-off and make her think twice.'

'It'll take her a lot more to believe anything I tell her now,' objected Jyp miserably.

'Cheer up,' ordered his aunt, 'we find out soon enough – meanwhile from what you were telling me I should watch your step where Morris is concerned. Perhaps it would be safer if you kept away from the office for the next few days until we get an answer on this lot – I'll ring up and say you're sick, if you like.'

'No, better not,' answered Jyp thinking it over. 'It'll only make him more suspicious and he might make a bolt for it before we've got our proof.'

'If you say so.' His aunt turned the problem over and cautioned. 'Well, whatever you do, be careful. A man like that is likely to stop at nothing when he's got the prospect of a swagbag of jewels dangling at his fingertips.'

'Don't worry, I'll be extra careful for Julie's sake,' promised Jyp and the subject was dropped, although he was conscious they were stepping into dangerous waters.

* * *

Directly he returned to the office all his attempts to mend fences were met with such a frigid response he had the distinct impression that Morris had spent most of the lunch hour twisting the knife in Julie so much she regarded Jyp as some sort of a monster. Increasingly depressed by the oppressive atmosphere Jyp decided to visit Reg, and making his excuses with Patience made his way to the address she gave him.

Brightening at the prospect of relieving the boredom, Reg listened avidly to the latest office news and the importance of his discoveries and agreed with Jyp's aunt on her diagnosis of the situation.

'Listen Jyp, my old mate, I've seen some weird characters in my time but this Morris character sounds the worst of the lot – I should watch my step, if I were you.' Your aunt was dead right – is there anything you can do to stay away from the office until she comes up with the goods? Sounds as if that Morris will do anything to get his mitts on those gems of Miss Julie's.'

'I'll try to think of something, but how are you getting on?'

'Don't worry about me. This little chat of ours has done me the world of good. I'll be back in the office as soon as I can and keep an eye on things. Just keep me posted.'

'I will. I don't think he will dare do anything while both of us are there. Meanwhile, I think I'll take the rest of the afternoon off and get ready for whatever tomorrow brings – whatever mood he's in.'

* * *

Similar concerns were currently being viewed at the highest level, after a wide ranging review in the inner recesses of Whitehall.

'I say, Binky old chap have you heard the latest?'

'I know, isn't it dreadful.'

'Just as we thought we'd got it all sorted out – this had to happen.'

'I know, we did our best, but it wasn't good enough.'

'They should never have put him in.'

'He's blown it this time.'

'I don't suppose we'll be able to save it now. That's another one up the spout.'

'What we want is another fast hitter, with his eye on the ball.'

'Even a stone waller would be something to write home about.'

'What we need is a draw to give us time to pull our socks up.'

'Whatever happened to Freddie Truman?'

'It's never been the same since Denis Compton packed it in.'

'Never a truer word. Sickening, isn't it, when you think we invented the blessed game.'

'It's no good – let's think about more cheerful things.'

'At least we've still got that Morris chap putting up a good score down at Plumpton.'

'Steady on, old man – walls have ears.'

'Thank Heavens for small mercies. I say that was a brilliant stroke putting that man in – he'd have shown them a thing or two at the wicket, what?'

'I couldn't have put it better myself. We haven't had a whisper of anything going on down there these days.'

'I expect they're getting used to that smashing young secretary coming into all that money they were telling us about. They'll be queuing up to take her out now, I wouldn't be surprised. I wouldn't mind taking a pop at her myself.'

'I hope it doesn't upset the apple cart – we can't afford to lose either of them after that other hiccup.'

'If he goes on like this, we'll be putting him up for a gong of some sorts, what?'

'Wouldn't be surprised.'

'We couldn't have done better. I have the utmost faith in Morris – one of those steady, dependable fellows. Remind me to ring him up some time and see how he is.'

'Right ho, old chap. They don't make them like that any more – salt of the earth, bar none. Where would the British Empire have been without them?'

'I say, that reminds me, talking about bars – sun's over the yard arm, I see. Time for a quick one, eh?'

'Never a truer word – lead me to it, old chap.'

* * *

When Jyp arrived back home he felt so buffeted by the day's events all he wanted was a quiet night, to give him time to face up to whatever devious tricks Morris might spring on him in the morning. He sat down and watched a couple of cartoons involving a superman coming to the rescue of a kidnapped heroine before his aunt noticed his tired face and preoccupied air and instantly took charge.

'What you need is a hot bath and a good night's sleep. While you're having a soaking, I'll get some soup ready and it's off to bed with you, my lad. You'll have to do with my old towel for the moment, until the new one comes in.' She gave him a sympathetic pat, 'But seeing the state you're in I don't suppose that matters. Off you go – I'll be putting the soup on.'

Jyp needed no extra bidding. With a sigh of relief he ran the bath and lay back soaking in it blissfully. He would have been happy to stay there indefinitely but a shout from below brought him back to his senses, and fighting back a yawn and towelling himself reluctantly he donned a dressing gown and joined his aunt in the kitchen.

Putting down his spoon after the last mouthful, with another prodigious yawn Jyp excused himself and trailed upstairs, taking his towel with him to dry out on the back of a chair. Pulling back the bedclothes Jyp was grateful to see his aunt had slipped in a hot water bottle. As he sank back and relished the luxurious warmth he heard his aunt call up, 'Don't trip up over the football – it's come over from next door again. Oh, and I've left my old stick up there. If you want anything in the night just give it a bang on the floor.'

'Thanks, Aunt,' murmured Jyp drowsily and lay there staring dreamily at the ball sitting on the chair and the long bathroom towel draped over the back.

As he stared mesmerised by the ball, waves of sleep began to wash over him and he began to drift effortlessly and felt himself being lifted and transported in a succession of changing scenes, from the countryside to the street of London and up the steps of Downing Street, arriving at a door marked 'Cabinet Office'. Inside, a row of elderly statesmen were seated in a row waiting expectantly, and the image of a football that had stayed firmly imprinted in his mind was replaced by the august features of the Home Secretary.

While he hesitated the face in front of him lost its severity and managed a welcoming smile. 'Don't stand on ceremony – sit down, my boy.'

Jyp obeyed and sat there anxiously. What had he done to deserve this, he thought feverishly.

Noting his unease, the man heading the meeting broke the silence, 'You may have wondered why we asked you to attend this special gathering?'

Jyp swallowed. 'Yes, sir.'

Before going on, the official glanced around his colleagues seeking confirmation and, reassured, continued, 'You can be certain we would not have considered such an action unless the matter had been of the highest national priority.' He coughed, 'If I might explain, Prime Minister.'

'Yes, yes, get on with it,' the PM consulted his watch, 'we may be too late already.'

'Quite so.' His cabinet colleague turned to Jyp. 'This must, of course, be treated as highly confidential because of the gravity of the situation and must not on any account go beyond these four walls. I have your complete assurance on this?'

'Of course,' Jyp answered, his voice drying up, overcome by the seriousness of the occasion.

'Right.' He unfolded a map and traced a route. 'At this very moment, a large fleet of enemy warships are entering the English Channel intent on invading our country and the only defence we have to resist them is a frigate that is already due for de-commissioning.'

Following a furious nodding of heads from the others, he added quickly, 'Naturally, our men are of the highest calibre and are ready to fight to the last man, as one would expect, but there is an added complication.'

'Yes?' Jyp asked weakly.

The official appealed to the others and the PM barked, 'For Heavens sake get on with it - otherwise we'll be here all night, man.'

'The thing is,' he swallowed, 'they are holding to ransom the daughter of one of our most prominent officials who does not want to be identified,' another quick glance around, 'and they say if we do not agree to their demands she will not be allowed to go free.' He ran a finger across his throat expressively. At his words, a mixed reaction of horror and outrage echoed around the room.

Jyp stared at each of them in turn, his eagerness fading, hoping that someone would have the answer – any answer. 'Isn't there anyone you can call on to help?' As he spoke, he found himself the target of a row of eyes boring into him, their faces looking remarkably like the shop owners he had encountered outside his office.

The PM got to his feet and patted him on the back heartily, while the others crowded around excitedly. 'Exactly, I knew you would have the answer – when can you start?'

'Me? You can't mean...' he scrambled to his feet, appalled at the prospect.

'Nonsense, of course we do.' The Home Secretary joined in, massaging his back affectionately. 'Is this the man who knows no fear? Our finest spy catcher - the one who laughs at danger and polishes off a couple of hundred before lunch, or so our friend, Brigadier Sleuth tells me?'

'No, no, it's all a mistake,' he found himself babbling. 'I only laid them out and added them up. I wouldn't know the first thing on how to go about it.'

'Say no more, we'll take care of all that, one hundred percent. Let me introduce you to our expert on spy gadgets, he'll put you in the picture – Major, um, whatever, he's a sound man. Over to you, Percy, I'll leave him in your good hands, buttons to push, and so forth.'

Left to their own devices Jyp was joined by a tall languid man who looked him up and down. 'Average height, mmm, what have we got, I wonder.' He rummaged in his satchel and produced a small metal clip. 'I should mention that some of this gear is still in the development stage, so we mustn't expect too much. However, this should do the trick.'

He motioned at Jyp's stick. 'I see you've already got a useful weapon there. Now if we clip this little gadget on and give it a fix to work on, that should get you there without any trouble.'

Jyp looked on bemused. 'And what do I do with it when I get there?'

The gadget man looked surprised. 'Oh, didn't they tell you? Why you just wade in and rescue the lady – I should have thought that was just down your street.'

'But-but.'

'Oh ah, I should have mentioned, silly me.' Percy peered into his satchel again and fished out a canister and screwed it on the end of the stick. 'That should do the trick. Just point it at the blighters and press this button. It'll bleep like a mobile, so you can't go wrong – that should take care of them. Oh, and I almost forgot, you'll need this invisibility cloak to give you an element of surprise – ah, I see you've already got one.' He picked up Jyp's bath towel and wrapped it around his neck. 'There you are.' He checked his watch. 'Here, it's time I was off – good luck and all that.'

'But supposing it doesn't work,' cried a panicked Jyp. 'What do I do - aren't you coming with me?'

'Good Heavens no, much too dangerous - I only develop the stuff. All you need to do is to hold it like this and bingo. Here, let me show you.' He leaned over and pressed a button.

There was a whirring noise and the stick jerked up.

As he felt himself being lifted into the air, Jyp shouted desperately, 'But how do I get back?'

Percy gave the thumbs up and pointed to another button, his voice almost lost in the roar of the motor revving up. 'Try that, at least I think that's the one.'

The last words Jyp heard before he rose up into the starlit sky was, 'Ah well, let's hope he has better luck than the last chap.'

Far above, Jyp was battling with the elements to keep on the flight path. Waves of sleep washed over him as he tried to work out where he was going and more importantly, how he managed to get himself into such an almighty mess in the first place.

Buffeted by the wind he at last felt himself being tipped onto a new course and managing to look down through a break in the clouds as he held on he was able to make out the outline of a warship far below.

What followed convinced him he was in the middle of a nightmare. As the deck rushed up towards him with frightening speed, Jyp shut his eyes instinctively and the next moment his feet hit the deck and all hell was let loose. His towel slipped off and as if by magic, a crowd of hostile figures appeared and ran towards him brandishing weapons. Remembering his last minute instructions, Jyp pointed his stick and pressed a button, setting off a bleep. Immediately, a stream of blue flame fanned out across the deck and the front ranks fell back, melting before him.

Unable to believe his eyes, Jyp plucked up courage and picked his way through the fallen bodies and mounted the stairs to the upper deck, peering into the compartments as he went.

His attention was drawn to some muffled cries coming from the last cabin and kicking the door open he came face to face with a face he recognised as the spy he had seen escaping on his nursery run - and behind him was his old enemy Charles Morris, guarding a figure lying bound up with ropes in the background.

Waving his stick, Jyp ordered 'Let her go!' hoping the tremble in his voice didn't show.

Jeering, Morris pointed a gun at his captive, 'Drop your weapon or she dies.'

Taking advantage of the situation, the nearest spy launched himself at Jyp unexpectedly, hoping to catch him off guard.

Instinctively, Jyp pushed him away and the man fell back, smothering Morris's aim.

At the same time his finger automatically tightened on the trigger blasting the two spies out of the way.

Dropping his stick Jyp fell on his knees, tugging at the rope until the captive was free.

Lifting her head to help her up, Jyp found himself gazing at his sweetheart, Julie.

'Quick, quick – before they come back,' she begged. 'They threatened to kill me.'

In the nick of time, Jyp remembered to press the right button as the door burst open.

* * *

But it was not the hostile ranks of the enemy that confronted him but an anxious auntie who shook his shoulder. 'Wake up Jyp, dear – do you know what time it is?'

'Mmmm?' Jyp shook his head, shaking off the lasting effects of his dream that were still vivid in his mind. 'Did they get her?'

'What are you talking about? Hurry up, or you'll be late for the office.'

Seeing the sluggish state he was in, she urged. 'Put a move on. I'll be getting your breakfast on while you dress.'

'Right.' He made an effort to throw back the bedclothes and half fell out of the bed. 'Be with you in half a sec.'

Eyeing him out of the corner of her eye as he tottered in later while she was turning the bacon over she asked, 'Are you sure you're all right to go to the office – you sound half asleep, dear.'

'I'm fine,' he insisted, nearly missing his mouth with the next helping.

'Well you don't look all right to me,' she observed. 'Have this cup of coffee to wake you up.'

He took a quick swallow and glancing at the time got to his feet hurriedly. 'Is that the time?

I'd better be off.'

His aunt shook her head. 'Well, for goodness sake be careful. If I know anything about that boss of yours, you'll need to watch your step. I tell you what,' as he got up to leave, 'why don't you take that old stick of mine – at least you've got something to defend yourself with in case he tries something.'

To keep her happy he slipped on his coat and picked up the stick obediently as he turned to leave. The feel of the knobbly surface brought back some strange memories. 'That's funny, I could have sworn...never mind,' he added hastily. 'I'll see you tonight as usual. Don't forget those checks you were making on you-know-who.'

'And you be careful, remember,' was her parting shot.

Chapter Thirteen

Nothing Too Strenuous

When he got to the office Jyp was half expecting a rocket for being late but nothing happened. He didn't bother to find out anything from Judie in view of the gulf that lay between them and instead sought out his friend Reg, after sheepishly depositing his stick behind his desk.

'All is quiet,' reported Reg without being asked. 'Can't understand it, mind you. He's been chasing us all around the block the past couple of days. 'Must be that girlfriend of his. No, not Miss Julie,' he forestalled the question hovering on Jyp's lips. 'That Simone piece – they've been on the phone like nobody's business lately. That means he's up to no good, you mark my words. Oh, and I've been asked to let you know that Miss Julie will be out of the office most of today – something to do with a visit to her solicitors about her legacy. She didn't tell you?'

Jyp shook his head glumly. 'We're still not on speaking terms.'

'Cheer up.' Reg tried to look on the bright side. 'She'll come round sooner or later when she's discovered what she's missed.'

'No such luck, I'm afraid. Oh well, I'd better go and see if there's any messages.'

'Don't worry, Patience will let you know if his nibs wants you,' said Reg, knowing what his friend meant. 'She's covering for Miss Julie until she gets back.'

As it happened, the call came sooner than he expected. No sooner had he sat down and looked through the post than a breathless Patience looked in.

'Oh, there you are, Jyp. The boss wants to see you right away. Sorry, I didn't hear you come in,' she added apologetically. 'I'd go right away, if I were you, he rang some time ago.'

But to his surprise, Morris gave no signs of being upset about anything. Instead, he invited Jyp to sit down while he finished off some correspondence. Then he sat back smiling and pulled out a file. Opening it, he studied it and apparently satisfied passed the top letter across.

'Now that you've passed your induction, so to speak, I think it's about time we gave you something to get your teeth into. Interested?'

Jyp nodded, waiting to hear what was in store. 'No more squatter's hand-outs?' he enquired politely and half jokingly, waiting to hear what was in store.

'Good Heavens no,' Morris assured him. 'Nothing too strenuous, I assure you. We've had a report from one of our reliable agents that some very interesting information has turned up at one of our safe houses. Here's the address. All you have to do is to pick it up. I can't rely on my usual contact because he's tied up on something else. Right?'

'Sounds ok,' replied Jyp cautiously. 'Do I have to identify myself?'

'No, nothing like that. I've arranged for it to be left just inside the front door on the mat.

Simple as that. Any questions?'

'No,' agreed Jyp. When do you want me to do it?'

'Nothing like the present,' replied Morris blandly. 'I'd go myself if I wasn't expecting an urgent call.' He rose to his feet. 'Oh, and you'd better memorise the address and let me have that back before you go, just in case.'

Jyp glanced at the letter as he got up. 'Right, I'll go right away - I'll just let Patience know.'

'No need – I'll see to that,' lied Morris smoothly. 'I've got one or two letters for her.'

'Right,' repeated Jyp, making a mental note to check with Reg just in case. Forgetting about the instructions he was given about leaving the address behind, he tucked it in his pocket after leaving the office and immediately sought out his friend and told him about his latest assignment.

'Sounds fishy to me,' was his friend's instant reaction. 'I should watch my step, if I were you. That man wouldn't have sent you off like that just to pick up some information when it's only ten minutes or so away in a taxi - it doesn't make sense.'

'Don't worry,' Jyp gave a short laugh, 'the same thought had occurred to me.' He hesitated and came to a decision. It was time to let his friend know the true facts about the situation and he proceeded to bring him up to date about the steps that he and Aunt Cis had already taken.

'You see, until my aunt comes up with the proof, we're stumped. If he turns out to be who Aunt Cis thinks he is, he's the one who's been behind all these security failures we've been having. He's not only set them up but he's been extracting blackmail from all the other managers we've been stuck with, to make sure they do as they're told. All we need now is for Aunt Cis to prove he's the man who signs himself "C".' He took a deep breath. 'I've decided we can't wait any longer, especially with all that money of Julie's involved - so I'm going to stick my neck out and see if he takes the bait.'

'Like a sitting duck?' questioned Reg dubiously. 'In that case,' he handed over his mobile, 'why don't you take this with you. You never know when you might need some help. Don't hesitate if things get sticky.'

'Thanks.' Jyp tucked it away. 'I'll do just that. Oh, and make a note of the address, just in case. Wish me luck.'

'It's all yours,' promised Reg. 'Meanwhile, I'll get Patience to keep an eye on his nibs.'

'The only way to find out what he's up to is to tape his calls, particularly where Julie's concerned,' replied Jyp sadly. 'She won't listen to me.'

'Why didn't I think of that?' agreed Reg. 'I'll get Patience onto it, don't worry.'

Watching Jyp go, he shook his head. Why two normally rational people should behave like that over money was beyond his comprehension. After explaining things to Patience his attention was caught by an insistent ringing at the front door.

Heaving himself to his feet he made his way to the shop door, waving Patience away as he went. 'Don't worry, luv, I'll see to it.'

When he got there a messenger was waiting on the doorstep, holding a large package in his hands.

Special delivery for,' he consulted his list, 'a Miss Julie Diamond.'

Reg was about to say Julie was out when he recognised it was the package they were expecting. He quickly took the pad out of the messenger's hands and scribbled a signature. 'That's all right, I'll sign for it.'

The messenger stood there undecided. 'I was told to ask for her especially, sir.'

Well, I'm sorry, she's out at the moment, but I'll see that she gets it directly she's back,' promised Reg. 'I'm her personal assistant,' he fibbed, crossing his fingers behind his back.

'That's all right then.' The messenger tucked away his pad, satisfied.

After he had gone Reg took a closer look at the package and whistled to himself. 'I wonder if this could be something to do with Miss Julie's inheritance.' He gently shook it and pondered. With Jyp out of the way, there was nothing to stop his nibs making off with it.

There was only one way to make sure. He tucked it under his arm and cautiously made for the top of the stairs. Just as he started to open the door, a familiar voice stopped him in his tracks.

'You there – is Miss Julie back yet?'

Reg jumped and hurriedly slipped the package hopefully out of sight behind the door as he turned, trying to keep his voice steady. 'No sir, not yet.'

'Oh, and Miss Julie told me she is expecting a delivery shortly - let me know when it arrives so that I can look after it. Damn it, there goes my call.'

Reg wiped his forehead and escaped while he had the chance.

Closing the door behind him to make sure he was undisturbed, Morris snatched up the phone. 'Yes?' he barked. 'Oh, it's you. At last.' He sat down abruptly. 'Where have you been? Listen, there's no time to waste. He's on his way, yes he should be there any minute. Make sure you've got the place wired up. Yes, as soon as he enters. Well, make sure you get it right this time – and don't forget to ring me afterwards and let me know.' He slammed the phone down and drummed his fingers on the desk impatiently.

* * *

Unaware of the fate that awaited him Jyp paid off the taxi and stood peering along the row of terraced houses, trying to figure out which house it was he was supposed to visit. Pulling out the scrap of paper he repeated the address to himself again. 'Let me see, what was that number again? Was it 16 or 91?' He turned the paper around and studied it from different angles. It's no good, he admitted candidly to himself, let's face it, you're hopeless at numbers.

Stopping at the nearest house he checked the number and was just able to make out the outline of the figure twelve on the gate, despite the peeling paintwork. Right, he decided, if it's sixteen we want, it should be along here. Ah, this must be it. He stopped and was about to turn in at the gate when he caught sight of a car drawing up on the other side of the road. A man got out who he immediately recognised - it was the same one who scarpered when he was doing that school run.

Drawing back behind a bush Jyp watched as the man went into a house opposite, carrying a case with wires hanging out at the side. That does it, it must be the one, he decided – it's 91, not 16. He waited until the man came out again some time later without the case and watched him as he sat in the car, glancing at his watch every few minutes.

What on earth's going on? Jyp pondered. *He must have been waiting for me to turn up – what's he up to?* The answer came from an unexpected quarter as a post office van suddenly pulled up outside and a postman climbed up the steps to the front door, thumbing through his deliveries as he went. Immediately, the man in the car threw away his cigarette and jumping out, darted up the steps and grabbed hold of the postman. Taken by surprise, the postman pulled his arm away and did his best to carry on with the man hanging on in a mad panic, trying to stop him.

Without thinking Jyp decided to cross the road to give a hand. But he had not reckoned on the stubborn qualities of the British postman. Pulling himself free, the postman picked out the parcel he was intending to deliver and threw it through the open doorway.

Jyp was about to rush to help when he was pulled up short by an insistent ringing on the mobile that Reg had thrust on him before he left. Remembering his dream last night of battling with the enemy he instinctively raised his stick in response when a thunderous ball of fire and smoke erupted from the house in front of them, snatching away the two men in front of him and engulfing him in a billowing cloud of acrid smoke. As the haze cleared a stray brick caught Jyp a glancing blow on his forehead sending him reeling. Steadying himself, he regarded his stick with an awed look of disbelief before a second brick hit him and he slumped to the ground unconscious.

* * *

Back at the office the manager was caught up in a fever of suspense. As the minutes ticked by it began to sink in that the absence of any message from his sidekick could mean only one thing – his main threat had been eliminated. Morris glanced at his watch. It was cutting it fine, but if the parcel had arrived there was still time to put his plan into operation.

Peering out of his office he glanced in the reception area and caught sight of a package leaning against Julie's desk. He rubbed his hands and dived back into his office.

Checking his timetable he snatched up the phone and got through to the operator. Once he was connected, he spoke urgently with a note of triumph. 'Is that you Simone? Yes, Charles, your lover boy, of course.' His eyes glistened with anticipation. 'Listen. You remember that fake story we cooked up about you and Jefferson in that hotel bed, well we don't need that any more - I've got rid of that menace at last. Yes, he fell for it, walked right into it. I haven't heard back, so our contact must have copped it as well. So you can pack your bags. What? Yes, it's here, I've just looked. We're in the money at last. No, she's out, no problem. I promised her I'd look after it until she got back. D'you know what, the silly girl believed me - imagine that! By the time we've finished with those little beauties, nobody will recognise them. Yes, they're worth a bundle. No more spying for yours truly – it's a mug's game.Listen, I'll meet you at the airport in half an hour – you know where. Bye.'

Grabbing his passport and wallet he stuffed them into his overcoat and slinging it over his shoulders cast a last triumphant look around before leaving.

'So long, suckers,' he saluted, then humming to himself made tracks for the entrance. He was about to pick up the eagerly awaited parcel when he was confronted by the unexpected appearance of Reg.

He halted, cursing under his breath, then recovering he adopted a hearty approach. 'Ah, just the man I was looking for. That's Miss Julie's delivery, I see. Good, excellent, I'll see to that.'

Reaching out to pick it up he was forestalled by Reg who took up a defensive position, blocking off his attempts to retrieve it. 'Excuse me, sir, but Miss Julie gave me explicit instructions to guard it until she arrived.'

Morris breathed heavily. 'Explicit instructions, did she?'

'Yes sir, those were her very words,' replied Reg firmly, hoping it would put the other off from examining the parcel too closely.

Morris thought furiously. 'Well, she spoke to me on the phone only a few minutes ago and asked me to drop it in to her on the way. Now, out of the way, man, I've got an important meeting to go to and I'm running out of time.'

'Oh, well that's all right then.'

As Reg allowed himself to waver Morris took the opportunity of elbowing him out of the way and snatched up the parcel, giving it only a cursory glance as he made for the door.

'I'll take full responsibility,' he called out impatiently over his shoulder.

'You do that,' Reg said to himself, 'and a fat lot of good it will do you. Now let's see what Patience has managed to find out.'

'You'll never believe this,' she waved excitedly at him. 'Come and listen.'

As she switched the playback on the smartphone they caught the opening words, 'Is that you, Simone? Yes, Charles, your lover boy,' when they were interrupted by a furious pounding on the shop door below. They looked at each other in wild surmise.

Reg was the first to speak. 'Don't say he's found out.' He waved his hand at the smartphone. 'Switch that thing off while I go and see.'

Hurrying to the entrance, he started to pull back the bolt but before he could open the door it was pushed open and Julie fell in.

'What's the idea locking up at this time of the day – has there been a break-in or something?'

'No, Miss,' he apologised. 'Sorry about that, but there's been quite a lot going on while you've been out of the office.'

Julie allowed herself to be ushered in, looking bewildered. 'I don't understand – Charles passed me just now in such a hurry, he didn't even say hello.'

'I think you'd better come in and hear all about it, Miss,' said Reg tactfully, not quite sure how to break the news.

When they got back to the office Reg shrugged his shoulders helplessly at Patience and pulled a chair out. 'I think you should sit down, Miss, for a minute – this might come as a bit of a shock.'

Julie glanced wonderingly at him and obeyed, sitting down abruptly. 'What's this all about?'

Reg heaved a sigh and nodded at Patience to switch on the recording.

There was a spluttering noise and suddenly the voice started with a jerk and Julie winced at the revelation about the hotel episode. 'Oh Jyp, what a fool I've been,' and burst into tears. In doing so, she completely missed some of the following words as the implications began to sink in. 'It can't be.' She appealed to Reg. 'What does he mean, "he got rid of him", he can't mean Jyp?'

Reg nodded sadly and admitted, 'There's a lot Jyp didn't tell you because,' he hesitated, 'he thought you would find it difficult to believe.'

'Go on.' She wiped her eyes and sat back, ready to hear the worst.

'Well,' he collected his thoughts, wondering how to put it into words, 'he found out that Morris wasn't telling us the truth about his background.'

'I know,' interrupted Julie tearfully, 'that's what he was trying to tell me and I didn't believe him.'

Deciding it was time to come clean Reg took a deep breath and plunged in. 'He passed on all the bits of information about Morris to his aunt, including a photo we had done around the table that his aunt wanted for identification purposes and when he realised what we'd done he had me beaten up on the way in so's he could get it back.' He waited while Julie dabbed her eyes again. 'Apparently, Jyp's aunt was in the same game as we are before she retired,' he explained.

'I didn't know that.' Julie sat up, suddenly interested.

'Yes, we didn't know either,' Reg agreed. 'Anyway, what with the photo and everything, she found out that he was well known for being fond of the ladies and he had a way with them, if you know what I mean.'

'Yes, I know exactly,' Julie said ruefully.

'Apparently, Jyp found a sample of his writing that he was hoping would match up with a note he had written blackmailing Grimshaw.'

'And did it?'

'We don't know yet – that's what Jyp was waiting to prove.'

Julie gave a despairing wail. 'Why didn't he tell us?'

Reg looked uncomfortable. 'When he heard you had come into all that money, he realised it was only a matter of time before Morris, um, got hold of that parcel of yours and scooped the jackpot, and he decided to do something about it. At least we've ... ' he was about to add 'we've managed to dealt with that problem,' when Julie butted in.

'Never mind about the parcel, what has he done?' she broke off. 'And what did Morris mean about "he walked right into it...?" '

Reg said simply. 'Jyp decided not to wait. That's why he took a chance and went on that assignment, hoping it would flush Morris out.'

Julie closed her eyes. 'Oh my God.' Looking back over events she admitted miserably, 'It looks as if I've been a complete idiot.' Then waking up to the terrifying possibilities, she caught hold of his arm. 'Where did he go – he must have told you?'

Reg searched his pockets. 'Yes Miss, I've got it here somewhere. What did I do with it?'

'Surely you remember – what was the address he gave you?'

Digging deeper, Reg started to get worried. 'It was something to do with trees, I think.'

'Was it oak?'

'No, something different.'

'Ash, was it elm?'

'No, keep trying.'

'Sycamore, birch then?'

'Not quite, it'll come to me in a minute.'

Losing patience, Julie insisted, 'We can't wait. For Heaven's sake, let me have your coat. I'll find it.'

Reg handed it over and Julie after a quick inspection took command. 'Nothing here. What about your shirt pocket, no, what about your trousers, here, get them off.'

'Steady on Miss, ladies present.' As he complied reluctantly, Patience stared, her eyes opening wide at what was going on.

'No, nothing there either.'

Crossing his hands in front of him, Reg looked bashful. 'Can I have my things back now?'

'Never mind about your clothes – where's that address?'

'Miss, please Miss, I'm getting cold.'

But not everyone seemed to mind. Patience for one was revelling in the spectacle and drank him in, as if seeing him for the first time. 'Oh, Reg, you look so handsome.'

At her words, he looked up hopefully. 'D'you really think so?'

'Mmm.' She ran her hands over his chest lovingly. 'I've never seen you like this before.

You look so different with your clothes on.'

'I do?'

'Oh, yes,' she sighed romantically. 'Why didn't you tell me?'

'I didn't know you really cared.'

'You silly boy, of course I do. I knew you were the one, the first time I saw you.'

Reg caught his breath. 'Did you really?'

'Oh, yes, the others didn't mean a thing.'

'Not even my mate, Jyp?'

'Silly boy – he was our best man.'

'Does that mean, do you think you could ever?'

'Marry me? Oh, Reg darling, I thought you'd never ask.'

'Oh bliss!' Taking his courage in both hands he clasped her to him in the grip he had demonstrated so many times to his golfing customers.

Pleased as she was that yet another romantic problem on her list was sorted to the satisfaction of all concerned, Julie did her best to bring them back to reality.

'That's all very well, but what about that address?'

'Oh, sorry, Miss, I forgot.' He bestowed a loving glance at his intended. 'Let me think.'

'What did you do after he gave it to you?'

'Well, I went to answer the door to take delivery of that...'

'Never mind that, what happened after?'

'I took it downstairs while I decided what to do with it, and yes, I remember now. It was getting in the way, so, that's right, I popped it in the pocket of one of the golfing models while I dealt with the par...'

But Julie didn't wait any longer. She had heard enough. With a flash she was through the door and pounding down the stairs, two at a time, eager to lay her hands on the missing address. Rifling through the pockets, she seized on a strip of paper and ran back, waving it triumphantly in front of her.

'I've got it!'

Smoothing out the slip, she scanned it with bewilderment. 'What's this? 91, Arcadia Avenue? I thought you said it was something to do with trees?'

'Well, I knew it was something to do with some kind of rustic retreat, so I thought it must be trees.'

'You idiot!' cried Julie. 'Never mind, we've got it. You sure this is the one?'

Reg looked abashed. 'Yes, I remember it now. Miss, can I have my things back now?'

Julie was about to reply when there was a furious knocking on the door below. Without thinking, she said automatically. 'Answer that, Reg, while I think.'

Seeing his embarrassment, Patience took pity. 'Don't worry, I'll go. You get dressed, luv.'

While she was waiting, her thoughts tumbling madly around in her head, Julie snapped her fingers and picking up the phone, ordered a taxi.

After a rapid exchange of conversation below, the tousled figure of Jyp's aunt appeared panting at the effort of climbing the stairs, followed closely behind by Reg.

'Jyp's aunt, Miss,' he gasped. 'I don't think you've met. I was just explaining...'

'Never mind the explanation,' ordered Aunt Cis, cutting him short. 'No time for that. I gather you're Julie?'

'Pleased to meet you,' said Julie in turn. 'Has Reg told you?'

'Yes – you've got the address?'

Infected by the urgency, Julie nodded. 'I've ordered a cab.'

'Good, then we can wait for the taxi downstairs. I'll explain everything on the way.'

As they gathered their coats and made for the door Reg called out.
'Here, wait for me!

I'm coming too.'

Turning back, Julie gestured impatiently. 'Well, put a move on.'

'But, I'm not dressed!'

'Never mind that, you can do that in the taxi. Come on.'

Chapter Fourteen

I See No Trees

'So you see, Jyp was right all along,' ended Aunt Cis reprovingly as they settled themselves. 'It turned out that Morris and 'C' were the same man. He was blackmailing Grimshaw about his murky past – nothing to do with spying - he was just a crook, out for all he could get.'

'And I fell for it,' confessed Julie ruefully.

'And on top of all his philandering, he turned out to be married, as Jyp suspected when he saw the mark left by a ring on his finger.'

'And I didn't believe him. Oh, Jyp love, what a fool I've been.'

'Never mind,' consoled Aunt Cis. 'I don't expect you were the only one.'

Having delivered her judgement, she shifted to make herself more comfortable. 'Move over, chaps,'she appealed. 'It's a bit of a squash in here.'

'Yes,' said Julie, trying to straighten up. 'Do you mind removing your elbow, Reg, dear?'

'Sorry, Miss. I'm trying to get my shirt on.'

After much heaving, a muffled voice made itself heard. 'You've just managed to pull it over my head, young man,' complained Aunt Cis from underneath. 'And watch my hair, if you don't mind. I haven't got much these days, but I'd prefer to hang on to what's left.'

'Sorry, is that better?'

'Well, it would be if you could help me get my foot out of your trousers.'

'I thought it looked funny down there. Sorry, Aunt Cis.'

'Never mind, young man, it's been in funnier places in its time. While we're at it, will someone tell the cabby where we're going?'

'Yes, where's that address?' exclaimed Julie anxiously. 'I should have it somewhere. Oh, here it is.' She reached forward and pushed back the partition. '91, Arcadia Avenue, please.'

'Blimey, you'll be lucky,' commented the cabby cheerfully. 'It's all hell let loose down there – rossers all over the place.'

'The police?' Aunt Cis leaned forward alertly. 'Why's that?'

'Some sort of panic, I expect. What with all these terrorists around these days, you never know what to expect.'

As they approached the avenue Julie leaned forward and read the road sign. 'This looks like it,' she told the others, keeping her eye on the numbers as they passed the neat rows of houses. Then with a dig at Reg, noting the absence of any signs of shrubs along the front, she couldn't help adding, 'I see no trees.' In doing so, she followed the tradition set by Horatio Nelson who turned a blind eye to his orders to withdraw at the Battle of Copenhagen, with the words 'I see no ships'. But Julie was filled with a different mission, equally determined to succeed in finding out what had happened to Jyp.

Still trying to get dressed in what little space there was available, whilst untangling himself from his underwear, Reg looked mortified. 'I couldn't help it, Miss – I was only thinking of a cosy retreat. Somewhere nice and quiet to live, with Patience, like.'

Feeling slightly guilty at the reproachful tone of his voice, Julie apologised. 'I do understand. I'm sure you'll find what you want after this is over.'

But as the road ahead showed increasing signs of disorder, with bricks and lumps of mortar strewn across the road, Julie's thoughts turned to more immediate problems.

'What's up, cabby?'

'Looks like we're heading right into it, luv,' answered the driver, slowing up. His assessment turned out to be accurate when they made out a hazard warning ahead and a policeman directing traffic.

'Look out!' warned Aunt Cis. 'Looks like a road block ahead.'

'Crickey, you're right, Missus, this is Arcadia Avenue all right – what's left of it.' He stuck his head out of the window. 'What's up, mate?'

A stern face appeared at the window. Their hopes subsided. It was their old enemy, Inspector Grooch. Waving them down, his voice took on a commanding note as he puffed himself up importantly. 'I'm afraid this road is closed, Madam.'

The cabby closed his eyes expressively. 'I can see that mate – how do we get through?'

'Don't you use that tone of voice to me – I am not your mate,' the Inspector snorted, his normally carefully groomed appearance spoilt by a somewhat crumpled uniform and a smear of what looked like coal dust on his face. Straightening up his spectacles that were hanging slightly askew, he peered more closely at the occupants. 'Ah, Miss Diamond, I didn't realise it was you. I regret this road is closed until further notice.'

Julie leaned forward, concerned. 'Why, what's up, Inspector?'

'I'm afraid I'm not at liberty to say.' His voice took on a pompous air. 'Suffice it to say, I've had strict orders to divert traffic away from this immediate area.'

Julie tried a sympathetic approach. 'It must be something serious – you look as if you've been in the thick of it.'

'Ah, thank you, Miss – we've all had our cross to bear. It's pretty sticky ahead. There's a lot of nasty stuff hanging around still.'

'And we all know what that is,' murmured Aunt Ciss in the background.

Stiffening up, the Inspector took in her companion. 'Ah, Mrs Green, I might have known you'd be popping up somewhere or other.'

Ignoring his comment, Julie placated him in an effort to find out more. 'I'm sure you must be doing your best in a difficult situation, Inspector – but can't you just tell us what's happened?'

Unbending, the Inspector looked over his shoulder and lowered his voice. 'All I can tell you, Miss, is that there has been a kind of, ahem, explosion in one of the premises along the road and one or two casualties.'

'Casualties?' The word caught in Julie's throat. 'What sort of casualties?'

The Inspector took a step back at the force of her question. 'That I am not liberty to say, Miss.'

'You mean you don't know,' was Aunt Cis's withering verdict.

Stung, the Inspector straightened his spectacles and said reluctantly, 'All I can say, Miss, is that the Medics have been in attendance and the injured have been taken to the Cottage Hospital.'

'How do we get there?' Seeing the indecision on the Inspector's face, Julie added quickly, 'It's urgent, we think our friend may be involved.'

Recalling his position, the Inspector replied stolidly, 'I'm sorry I can't help you there. If you retrace your route back to the main road, Miss, I'm sure someone may be able to direct you.'

Tired of listening to the exchanges, the cabby leant out. 'What you on about, mate? This road is the quickest way of getting there. Blimey, it's only the other end of the street.'

Irritated, the Inspector drew himself up. 'That's enough of that. Any more lip from you, young man and I'll report you to the proper authorities. What's your number?'

The cabby blew a raspberry.

'What did you say?'

To divert attention, Aunt Cis leaned forward confidentially, 'A word in your ear, Inspector Grouch.'

'Grooch, if you don't mind, Madam.' The inspector stiffened up, affronted.

'Grooch then. Listen, this mustn't go any further...top security.'

The Inspector unbent slightly. 'Security? Is this something I should know about? Why hasn't anyone told me?'

Aunt Cis winked an eye at the others and replied smoothly. 'This on a need-to-know basis, you understand.'

'Ar, um,' he eyed her suspiciously. 'What is it you wish to tell me, Mrs Green?'

'It's all hush-hush. One of our security people was on a visit there this afternoon and hasn't reported back. We need to speak to him as soon as possible.'

Chewing his lip and trying to measure her up to his own idea of what a security official should look like, the Inspector twirled his non-existent moustache disapprovingly. 'Are you trying to tell me that you are some sort of a spook? I believe that's what they like to call themselves on the television medium these days. All that skulking behind the scenes - not what I would call the British way of doing things,' he snorted. 'Discipline and order – that's what made the British Empire what it is today.' He eyed her sternly. 'May I see your authority to substantiate such a statement?'

With a flash of inspiration, Aunt Cis produced a battered old security pass that had seen better days, being careful to cover up the corner of the card showing a date.

The Inspector's eyes opened in almost comical disbelief. 'Bless my soul, what's this?'

At the sight of the signature he straightened up, snapped his heels together with a salute, and handed it back reverently, nearly falling over in the process. 'Why didn't you say so in the first place, Madam. We're all try to do our little bit, so to speak, on behalf of the King and Country...I mean the Queen, of course.' He stood back and called out, 'Constable, wherever you are - at the double. Where the devil is the man, just when I want him. Oh, there you are.'

Mishearing where the voice came from, the despatch rider revved up and butted him from behind. 'Yes, sir?'

'Not in my back, blast you.' The flustered Inspector straightened his spectacles that had slipped and jammed against his chest. 'Look where you're going, idiot.'

'Sorry, sir. Your helmet, sir.'

Squashing it back on his balding head, the Inspector cleared his throat. 'Escort this party to the Cottage Hospital immediately. No, not that way - along Arcadia Avenue.'

'But you said...'

'Never mind what I said – this is an emergency.'

'Ok, you're the boss, I mean, sir.'

Rejoining the others the Inspector saluted deferentially. 'My man will see you through safely to your destination, Ma'am.' Stepping back, he saluted again. 'I don't think you will find us failing in our duty when the time comes, Ma'am.' He stuck his head in the window nearly getting his tie caught up as they moved off. 'In case you forget it, the name is Grooch, Ma'am.'

Sitting back with a sigh of relief Aunt Cis commented, 'Pompous ass – as if we're likely to forget.'

'Well, at least it did the trick,' Julie laughed, forgetting her worries for the moment. 'How did you manage that?'

'Oh, I just waved my old pass at him - good thing he didn't look at it too closely.'

'Why's that?'

'It's out of date,' she hooted. 'It should have handed it in years ago. Oh, my goodness,' she sobered up, as the car started bumping over some debris, 'it's beginning to look like a battleground along here.'

'Oh, my God – look at that!'

The despatch rider in front started to slow up, waving them down and they all craned their heads as they passed what was left of the next house in the row, taking in what remained left of the blackened windows and empty void where the front door had been.

'Crumbs, that must have been number 91,' muttered Reg, doing a swift calculation.

'No!' Julie's heart was in her mouth as the significance of Morris's remarks sank in.

'This is what he meant when he said Jyp walked right into it!' She shot forward and thumped on the window in front. 'Can't we go any faster?'

The cabby was aggrieved. 'Give over, lady. I can't go any faster. It's the rosser in front who's holding us up. If it wasn't for him, we'd have been there by now.'

'Steady on,' cautioned Aunt Cis sympathetically. 'It won't be long now – it's just at the end of the road, they said.'

'You don't understand – I'll never forgive myself if anything's happened to him!' exclaimed Julie tearfully.

Then they were past and in the clear and the road ahead was empty again.

'Here we are, Missus,' the cabby suddenly announced as they swept into the parking area in front of the entrance, joining a queue behind a line of ambulances. Before they began to slow up, Julie was reaching out for the door handle, impatient to get out.

'Hang on a minute, Missus!' the cabby warned, but Julie couldn't wait. In a flash, she jumped out and was running for the entrance.

'Here, wait for me,' called out Aunt Cis, already trying to extricate herself from the back seat.

The cabby glanced over his shoulder. 'Some people can't wait a minute. I'll come and give you a hand.'

'You don't understand,' wailed Aunt Cis exasperated from the back. 'This blithering idiot has tied our shoe laces together – I can't move!'

'Sorry, Aunt Cis, I was trying to get my socks on – I wondered why my feet looked so small.'

'Blimey,' said the cabby with a sigh. 'I've come across some weird cases, but it's the first time anyone has got stuck in me cab – they usually can't get out fast enough when they see the bill.'

'Don't worry about the fare, I'll see to that,' fretted Aunt Cis. 'Just get me out of here, so's I can catch up with Julie.'

But Julie was in no mood to wait for anyone. She was speeding past the reception before the duty clerk had time to put down his paper and in a flash had disappeared down the corridor. Seeing the 'Accidents and Emergency' notice, Julie veered off left and came panting to a halt by the enquiry desk. 'Where's the casualty ward?'

Before the clerk had time to answer, she cried impatiently, 'Casualties – where do I find them?'

'What name?' asked the nurse unhurriedly, consulting her list.

'Jyp, I mean Jefferson, er…Patbottom,' got out Julie in a rush.

'I don't see his name here. When was he admitted?'

'Oh, for Heavens sake, I don't know…some time this morning, I think – what does it matter?'

'Well, unless I have his details,' began the nurse disapprovingly, then seeing the expression on Julie's face amended it soothingly to, 'what was the nature of his condition?'

Thrusting the recent harrowing picture of the shattered building and the gaping entrance from her mind, Julie blurted out, 'there was an explosion in Arcadia Avenue,' adding fearfully, 'I'm told you had some of the injured brought here.'

A glimpse of sympathy appeared on the nurse's face. 'Oh, those,' she said guardedly. 'Wait here and I'll ask Matron.'

Biting her lips Judie paced up and down waiting apprehensively. Then the Matron swept into view followed by the nurse.

'Miss Diamond?'

'Yes,' replied Julie automatically.

'Follow me, please.'

Keeping up with her brisk pace, Julie wondered how she had known.

Without explaining, Matron arrived at a cubicle and checking her list, swept the curtain aside revealing a mummified figure lying outstretched, bound from head to toe in bandages.

'I'll leave you to it. Try not to disturb him too much.' With a brisk nod of mission accomplished, she closed the curtain behind Julie and departed.

Julie took one look at the figure and flung herself at it sobbing.

'Oh Jyp darling, what have they done to you?'

At her touch, an eye opened slowly in wonder and a husky voice piped up. 'Am I dreaming? I must be in Heaven – I can hear an angel calling. Halleluya!'

Focusing on the unfamiliar voice, Julie sat up with a jerk. 'You're not Jyp! Who are you?'

Reciting as if on parade, the figure replied automatically. 'Postman Percy Smith, M'am, at your service, guaranteed delivery... except that last one, not sure what happened there.'

But Julie had heard enough. Springing to her feet she collided with the nurse who was hovering outside, checking her list. 'Sorry, Miss. Not quite sure how that occurred. Let me see, apart from these old boots they found.' She held up a pair that made Julie's heart contract, 'Ah, here we are, don't tell Matron. It may be that other patient in the next row you want. He's a lovely gentleman, but he's always telling me the wrong bed number – anyone would think he can't count.'

'Can't count?' repeated Julie with rising hope. 'Where is he?'

'I'll take you to him – promise you won't tell Matron, I'll never hear the last of it.'

'No, no, of course not. Lead me to him.'

'Bless you, Miss. He's just along here. There you are,'

Lifting the curtain she exclaimed, 'I thought so – number 16 and you told me 91, you naughty boy. See what I mean, Miss?' Pulling back the curtain she revealed the startled face of Jyp, half-hidden behind a bandage wrapped around his head.

'Jyp,' she sobbed throwing herself at the bed and cradling his head in her arms.

'Wha-at's happening!' His bewildered gaze took her in. 'I must be dreaming.'

'That's what the postman said,' said Julie gazing up at him lovingly. 'No, it's me and I don't care what you say – I'm here to stay, whether you like it or not. Will you ever forgive me for saying all those horrid things about you.'

'Of course,' he replied contentedly, drawing her closer. 'Whatever made you change your mind?'

'I was coming back to tell you, it didn't matter anyway, and then dear Reg managed to record those beastly telephone calls of Morris that he made to that awful snake in the grass, Simone, and how he planned to get rid of you, and he very nearly did. Oh, why did you go along with it? Dear God, I might have lost you - I can't bear to think about it.'

'Good man, Reg managed it, did he? It was the only way I could make him reveal his true colours,' explained Jyp soberly.

'He could have killed you,' wailed Julie, stroking his face.

'It was worth it, just to show you what he was up to.'

'Well, he'll never get the chance again and he's done a bunk anyway, so Reg tells me.'

'Good riddance.'

'And taken all my worldly wealth with him. Can you bear the thought, darling?'

Jyp sank back with a sigh of relief. 'That's all right then. Now if I could only go down on one knee.'

'Don't you dare move.' She pressed him back on the bed. 'What is it you want to do?'

'Only to propose marriage, Julie. You see, just before you got here...'

'Yes, I do!' she interrupted. 'I do!"

'Give me a moment, love. As I was saying, just before you got here Head Office decided to appoint me as the new Manager, so I've at last got something to offer you.'

'Didn't you hear what I was saying, you idiot? I don't care what job they give you, I just want you, for the rest of my life. Is that good enough?'

'Sounds good enough to me – go on, tell her, Jyp. Hurry up, because I've got some news for you,' Aunt Cis called out as she hobbled in, followed by Reg and then Patience close behind carrying a parcel.

Jyp looked bashful, conscious of his new audience. 'If you'll have me – yes.'

In a whoop, Julie snuggled in his arms, looking adoringly up at him. 'And I don't care if that man has stolen all that stuff of mine – I was going to give it away anyway. All I ever wanted was you.'

'Hang on, young lady,' announced Aunt Cis cheerfully. 'I should wait until you've heard what young Reg has come up with first.'

Reg stepped forward modestly. 'This was what I was trying to tell you about, Miss Julie, when you were rushing off. I managed to hide it away before he could get his hands on it. Show her, love.'

At the sight of the contents, Julie caught her breath. 'He didn't get away with them after all.'

She looked around bewildered. 'But what did he get?'

Reg tried to keep a straight face. 'It was a presentation set of golf balls I found down in the shop,' and joined in the general laughter.

Poking her head in to find out what all the noise was, the Matron coughed pointedly. 'I think the patient is getting over excited, if you don't mind. Only two visitors to a bed, rules are rules. 'That makes three of you,' she added for Jyp's benefit.

After she departed and Aunt Cis took the hint and led Reg out, Julie patted the bed for Patience to join her. 'I think I've found just the thing for your wedding present, my dear,' and delving into the parcel produced a small exquisitely shaped necklace.

Patience gasped. 'For me?'

Julie placed an arm affectionally around her shoulder. 'If it wasn't for you and Reg, my dear, I would never have realised how lucky we both were, in finding what we really wanted in life. And now it's up to Jyp to decide what he wants to do – whether to accept this new offer or...' She stared pensively into the distance. 'I wonder what they think of it all up in Whitehall, now that another of their trusted managers has let them down?'

Chapter Fifteen

We Never Make Mistakes

If she had been able to witness the effect it was having in Whitehall at that moment, she would have been reassured by the unrivalled ability of our civil servants to face the direst news with the utmost calm and equanimity.

'I say Binky, old man, what do you think about the latest? Bit of a cock-up, what?'

'Yes, that's the second time this week I haven't had my newspaper delivered – what's the world coming to?'

'I know, rotten bad show. I mean what are we going to do about, you know, that Morris chap? Seems we may have made some sort of a plonker there, what?'

'My dear chap, you must always remember that we never make mistakes in the Civil Service. We place our trust in what there is available. We can't be held accountable if they don't live up to our expectations.'

'No, no, of course not. You're absolutely right, old man.'

'Of course, we do have the occasional slip-ups, like not getting our newspaper on time.'

'I know, bad show that.'

'But, all in all, we manage to meet our targets.'

'Like setting up a sound management team to look after our security.'

'Hem, thank you for reminding me, Trevor, old man.'

'Not at all, Binky. Shoulder to shoulder, stick together, what.'

'Yes, how were we to know old Major Fanshaw was willing to swap state secrets for getting his green fees paid? We're not clairvoyant.'

'Or that Grimshaw blot was being blackmailed all because of that gym slip affair.'

'Absolutely not. Although I must say I was disappointed in old Morris. He seemed to have a lot going for him.'

'Half the women in England, by all accounts. A pity we didn't know about that Simone – I hear they nearly got stopped at Heathrow until she managed to show her credentials.'

'Yes, a nifty pair of pins, by all accounts. I bet he didn't tell her he was already married. You'd think old Morris would be grateful for getting away with it, though I hear he seemed more worried they were going to confiscate those golf balls they found on him. Seemed to think they were priceless, for some reason.'

'Perhaps he was looking forward to a game with old Fanshaw.'

'Never mind, at least we were able to rely on that Jyp fellow – that was a brilliant choice, Binky, if I might say so.'

'Yes, even if he went to that funny school you told me about – Watlingon County Grammar or something, wasn't it?'

'Well, we've all got to start somewhere, I suppose. What do we do about him? He seems to have put up a jolly good show. He managed to flush out old Morris even though that young Julie had given him the cold shoulder - that's enough to put anyone off.'

'Yes, it's a bit awkward, isn't it. I've offered him the job over taking over down there, but after everything he's been through he might decide he's had enough. I wouldn't blame him, what?'

'Tricky - very tricky. Of course, we could put him up for some sort of an award, for extraordinary courage and self sacrifice well beyond the call of duty, and all that rot.'

'Yes, what about a move upstairs, Binkey, old man? Ah, I've just remembered, we've put you up for that. Now, what can we say? Is he good at anything we can hang it on? Is he a good sportsman, or well known for something or other?'

His chief looked dubious. 'You were talking to him at that hotel reception. Did he give any clue we could use?'

Trevor thought back. 'Not a lot. Wait a minute, when we were talking to Morris, he did say something like he was counting on his new job to add up to something worthwhile.'

They looked at each other speculatively. 'Counting on his new job to add up to something? That's it. Of course.'

Binky smiled indulgently. 'I knew we would find the answer, if we put our mind to it. You'll see to that, will you, Trevor, old chap.'

'No worries – consider it done.'

'See you at the ceremony then.'

'Wouldn't miss it for the world.'

* * *

The day of the great event arrived. The sun was shining and as the hired car drew up to take them to Buckingham Palace, Julie made sure that Jyp looked his best despite the fact he was still wearing a bandage around his head.

'Are you sure I look all right?' he asked bashfully. 'I don't know why I said 'yes'- I must have been mad. There must be hundreds of others who should be getting an award.'

'Nonsense,' said Julie firmly. 'You owe it to your family and you deserve it, after all you went through.'

'But all I did was make that man Morris blow a hole in the front of that house – hardly grounds for an award. Reg should be getting a medal, not me. He was the one who managed to tape that evidence, not me.'

'Well, it's too late now to back out. Think of all the pleasure it will give our children when they grow up.'

'You sure you meant it when you agree to marry me, darling,' Jyp asked anxiously.

'Of course, I did you idiot. Mind you,' as the car turned into the courtyard, 'I might still change my mind if you start arguing about the money again. I can still give it all away.'

'I've stopped worrying about that,' confessed Jyp. 'As long as you'll still have me.'

'Idiot, come here.'

The next minute the door opened and the chauffeur coughed as he bent in to help them out. 'If I may suggest, sir, there is just a trace of lipstick, no, just to the right. We don't want his Highness seeing that, do we.'

Dabbing at his face, Jyp slipped a note in the chauffeur's hand and straightened up. 'No, You're dead right.' Turning to Julie he groaned, 'Oh my hat, there's my dad and what *is* Ma wearing?'

Julie tucked her arm in his and giggled. 'Don't go and spoil it for them, love, it's something they'll remember for the rest of their life.'

'Oh well, here we go.'

They joined a small line of couples ahead who were being ushered into the entrance.

The rest of the proceedings went in a confused blue as they were being directed to line up front of a raised platform, involving several attempts by the ushers to get him to take up the correct position.

When his turn came, Jyp nervously took a step forward and bowed his head. As he did so, the attendant intoned, 'The Order of the British Empire, for outstanding service in the realm of mathematics...'

His solemn announcement was interrupted by an hysterical outburst from someone at the back of the gallery.

The intervention seemed to amuse His Highness. 'Hello, someone seems a little overcome by it all. Is he a friend of yours?'

Jyp nodded his head embarrassed. 'My father, Your Highness.'

Making the presentation, His Highness smiled. 'Well, this should give him something to talk about.'

Before You Go

Before you go...If you could spare the time, it would make all the difference if you could add a few words of comment in the review section on the Amazon page, we'd love to hear from you. For more information, log on to the website, http://www.michaelwilton.co.uk/ http://www.michaelwilton.co.uk/ where you will find details of the stories currently available as well as news of forthcoming publications. Or go direct to Amazon:

https://www.amazon.co.uk/Michael-N.-Wilton/e/B00EPG3SF4

About The Author

Following National Service in the RAF Michael returned to banking, until an opportunity arose to pursue a career in writing. After working as a press officer for several electrical engineering companies, he was asked to set up a central press office as a group press officer for an engineering company before. From there he moved on to become publicity manager for a fixed wing and helicopter charter company, where he was involved in making a film of the company's activities at home and overseas.

He became so interested in filming that he joined up with a partner to make industrial films for several years, before ending his career handling research publicity for a national gas transmission company.

Since retiring he has fulfilled his dream of becoming a writer and has written two books for children as well as several romantic comedies.

You can read more about Michael on his website:

http://www.michaelwilton.co.uk/

Amazon:

https://www.amazon.co.uk/Michael-N.-Wilton/e/B00EPG3SF4

Books by Michael N Wilton

Save Our Shop

Losing his job at the local newspaper after depicting the sub-editor in a series of unflattering doodles, William Bridge is called on to help his uncle Albert keep his shop going. The first thing he does is fall in love with Sally, the latest shop volunteer, despite formidable opposition from her autocratic stepmother, Lady Courtney.

Following a break-in and lost orders, an SOS sent to Albert's maverick brother Neil for back-up support changes everything. On the run from the police, Neil disguises himself and encourages William to be nice to a visiting American security expert and his flighty daughter Veronica to promote business, causing a rift in the budding romance.

The pressure mounts for William to investigate rumours of a shady deal to take over the shop and threaten the life of the village. William is willing to pay almost any price in his desperate fight to win back his love and save the shop.

Amazon.com: https://www.amazon.com/dp/B00FRL6CEU
Amazon UK: https://www.amazon.co.uk/dp/B00FRL6CEU

In The Soup

Once again, William Bridge must put aside his ambitions to become a writer and marry his sweetheart Sally when her father, Sir Henry, is involved in a scandal that threatens to put an end to the family's hopes of getting their son Lancelot married to the daughter of a wealthy American security expert.

Foiled in his attempts to get his own back, Foxey Fred and his gang find a new way of retrieving their fortunes by blackmailing Sir Henry who, fearful his wife may find out, appeals to William for help. Calling on his Uncle Neil for support, William sets out to unravel the threads of lies and deceit despite continued opposition from Sally's stepmother, Lady Courtney, and a series of female encounters that are enough to test the trust of even the most faithful admirers.

Amazon.com: https://www.amazon.com/dp/B00YF2B87S
Amazon UK: https://www.amazon.co.uk/dp/B00YF2B87S

Happenings at Hookwood

Amazon.com:
https://www.amazon.com/dp/B00DU9SZ1E
Amazon.uk: https://www.amazon.co.uk/dp/B00DU9SZ1E

Grandad Bracey and the Flight to Seven Seas

Amazon.com: https://www.amazon.com/dp/B00CA51246
Amazon.uk: https://www.amazon.co.uk/dp/1326197282

Made in the USA
Monee, IL
22 August 2021

76255078R00104